MW01704986

Reflections & Echoes along the Path

DAVE + CINDY,
THANKS FOR YOU FRIENDSHIP!
BRIAN

BRIAN K. ROGERS

Reflections & Echoes along the Path

TATE PUBLISHING
AND ENTERPRISES, LLC

Published by Tate Publishing & Enterprises, LLC
127 E. Trade Center Terrace | Mustang, Oklahoma 73064 USA
1.888.361.9473 | www.tatepublishing.com

Tate Publishing is committed to excellence in the publishing industry. The company reflects the philosophy established by the founders, based on Psalm 68:11,
"The Lord gave the word and great was the company of those who published it."

Cover design by Gian philipp Rufin
Interior design by Jimmy Sevilleno

Published in the United States of America

ISBN: 978-1-63063-827-6
Fiction / Short Stories (single author)
14.02.18

DEDICATION

This book is dedicated to Joey, Theresa, Calla and Travis. Wherever you are, be careful! Love, Dad

Contents

Introduction

I AM A STUDENT of human nature. I am also someone who believes that the teachings of Jesus Christ are "The Way." They are the foundation of who I am. Jesus is my Lord and savior. But he is more than that to me. He is also my hero. If you were to ask me who my first choice would be if I could meet someone from the past, my answer is always the same: Jesus. No one inspires me more. The funny thing is it wasn't until I learned an awful lot about life before I realized it.

I went to college and took every religion and philosophy class I could take. I've read things from Kant, to Nietzsche, to Jung. I've learned about Buddhism, Islam, and Judaism. But no matter how far I roam from my center, it always leads back to Jesus, and my faith would become stronger and more secure than it was before. I am not preaching here or directing. I encourage everyone to search in any way they want to go. I'm confident you, too, will find your way, like a river that pulls us to the truth. But you needed to hear this from me to understand the nature of what you are about to read.

This book did not start out with this intention in mind. It started with an idea for a short story. Before long, another idea came to be, and soon I had what I felt was a good collection. Most of the people I need to thank are already in these stories in one way or another. It is my life, my passion that created this. When it comes right down to it, this book shows my soul. It is kind of scary that you might actually know me pretty well when you are done.

I truly hope that many times in this book you ask yourself: "What would I have done?" And then just maybe, this book will help you with your search. I hope you like it.

Audacious is the Heart that Burns

THE KING OF the dwarves had a reputation for being volatile. There was peace in the kingdom. *That was true,* thought Cam. *but it was only true because everyone was afraid of King Bork and what he might do.* The elves kept their distance and so did the ogres. The brownies ceded their northern forest just to keep Bork quiet. Very few would even approach the king, and that was where the problem lay for Cam. He was in love with the king's only daughter, Primacos.

Now Cam was a simple tradesman. He made barrels and sold them to the fishermen, on the coast and to the king's winery. He was the only cooper in the surrounding villages, so Cam was never "short" for work. That was a little play on words as Cam was only three feet tall. He was short, even for a dwarf, but that didn't really matter to him as Primacos was a few inches shorter.

Cam supplied the barrels for the King's winery and he would always deliver them himself. You see, Primacos ran the winery and it was the only way he could see her. The winery needed barrels once a week. Cam knew that Primacos worked on Tuesdays, so every Tuesday, Cam would make the delivery. And when he left, he would say, "See you next Tuesday," and they would laugh about it every time.

Primacos always seemed happy to see Cam, and Cam was always happy to see her. The problem was that she was very pretty and all the dwarves with money and power surrounded her. And Cam was just a simple tradesman. He sometimes wondered if she was only polite because she needed the barrels, but then he would remember her smile and how they always seemed to laugh on delivery day. He refused to believe anything bad about her.

And then one Tuesday, when Cam was unloading his wagon, his hand touched the hand of Primacos. It was an accident, but they both felt the specter of fate. Cam looked into her eyes and he saw love in there, and she marveled at the comfort she suddenly felt with him. *Father will not like this at all*, she suddenly realized. She knew right then that it was something she would have to fix.

Cam's confidence soared. He no longer worried about the little things that once seemed so important. He even felt he could confront the king himself. Primacos did not know how to tell him, so Cam decided to do it himself.

So, after his delivery the following Tuesday, Cam went straight to the castle. He wore his best clothes, but even so he felt he would not fit in. He went to the entrance of the king's great hall and found the door unguarded. He looked at the door and knew that only a short distance separated him from resolving the one thing that concerned Primacos the most. He knew he was supposed to get permission to enter, but the guard was nowhere to be found, so he cracked open the door and looked in. The main hall appeared empty. Cam stepped inside and slowly walked toward the empty throne. He marveled at the beauty and the craftsmanship of the room. He stood in front of the empty chair and wasn't sure how to proceed. Finding the great hall empty was not something he anticipated.

He turned to head back out, and suddenly he felt a sharp blow to his head, and everything swirled and went black. When he awoke an hour later, he found himself gagged and bound to a large pole in the back of the throne room. He was unable to speak or move. A guard stood nearby with a large spear. He stood at attention and appeared not to notice that Cam had awoken.

Soon he heard footsteps, and a dwarf wearing a great robe approached. When he saw the reflection of the silver crown, he knew it was the king. A smaller dwarf followed behind him and the two of them stared at Cam.

"Who is he?" asked the king.

The little dwarf replied, "He is the village cooper, sire."

The king nodded. He looked at Cam and said, "Do you know that it is a great crime to enter the throne room without permission? Only the royal family may come and go here. The penalty for this trespass is death. And since there are no exceptions to this law, there is no point in a discussion." He turned to the little dwarf. "Take him out of here and hang him immediately." Cam's eyes were wide open and sweat beads formed on his forehead. The gag in his mouth still prevented him from speaking.

Two guards rushed forward and lifted the pole out of the floor. They carried Cam right across the throne room like a pig for the feast and right toward the large door he came through. Just then the doors opened and Primacos entered followed by the village priest. She saw Cam tied to the pole and ordered the guards to stay where they were.

"Father, what are you doing?" The king sat on his throne and drank a glass of wine. He seemed annoyed at being questioned by his daughter as he sneered in her direction. "I'm going to hang this audacious cooper for trespassing…what does it look like?" Primacos started to object but her Father interrupted. "Since only the royal family can do what he did, there is no point of talking about it!" The king wasn't even aware of the irony that he was drinking the wine that was delivered by Cam.

"Father...he is a member of the royal family. We were married yesterday." The king jumped up from his throne and stepped halfway down the steps toward his daughter. "*What?*" he hollered. The priest stepped forward. "It is true, your highness," he said as he held out the marriage certificate to the king's aide. The king's assistant looked at it and nodded his verification to the king.

The king sat back down in a huff. He scratched his chin. He looked at the guards who stood by the pole with Cam restrained to it. The two soldiers both had their mouths open waiting for instructions. "Well? Don't just stand there like two idiots! Release him!"

The guards quickly untied him. Cam stood up and rubbed his wrists. Once the gag was removed, he rubbed his face. The king motioned for him to come forward. "Cooper...you are audacious...and very, very lucky!"

Cam nodded. "I intend to always be audacious in regard to your daughter, sire!" The king did not smile, but it was close.

He looked at his daughter. "Primacos, later we are going to have a long talk. But right now...we have a royal party to plan." He pointed to his aide, and the little dwarf ran out of the room to get things started. Cam and Primacos hugged and kissed in front of the throne. Now the king did smile, and the five guards that were in the room all began to clap.

Later that day, Cam and Primacos walked along the stream that ran to the winery. "Do you realize that was our first kiss?" said Cam. Primacos nodded yes. "Well, it wasn't a good-enough first kiss. I want a do over!" he said.

She laughed and said, "You are audacious! All right, I'll give you a do over, Cam!"

Cam laughed. "I'm audacious?" he chortled. "You lied about getting married to the king!"

Primacos smiled. "Well…It was the only way to save you. We'll get married later today and Father will never know."

Cam nodded. I'm going to miss telling you: "See you next Tuesday," he said. She laughed and said, "You can still say it…you'll just get to see me every day now!" The two dwarves held hands as they walked over a small wooden bridge. Later that day, the celebration began and it didn't end until the sun came up.

And from that day forward, King Bork lost his reputation for being mean. He eventually was known for being the best grandfather in the kingdom. And Cam and Primacos were happy…and audacious.

Barnyard Intrigue

THE HORSE WENT "nay," the cow went "moo," and the duck went "quack." It was a normal sort of morning on the farm. The sun started to lighten the sky, and the lack of clouds and the comfortable temperature indicated a pleasant morning was at hand, or hoof, depending on your perspective. The day began like it normally did with Barney the rooster crowing from the top of the long wooden barn. The sun was just now shining on the tops of the trees, and soon it would reach the ground. Not long after that, a light came on in the house bedroom and then another one in the kitchen. It was a clear indication that Barney had performed his job well once again.

Barney the rooster normally crowed a little late for those who live in the barn, but he did manage to wake up a few of the "over-sleepers." Maury the horse was already awake. He was a dark bay with a white spot in the middle of his forehead. He was uneasy this morning as he did not sleep well. He just could not seem to settle down. Charise, the farmer's prize pig, had her blue ribbon stolen the night before and the dark-brown bay with the white spot in the middle of his forehead did not like it one bit. Maury expected more than that from the farm animals. He was awake most of the night trying to determine who the culprit could be, but none of the farm animals had a motive to perpetrate such a heinous crime. What really bothered him was that everyone was a suspect...everyone, that is, but Barry. Barry was the only one who consistently stood above everyone else. He was the one animal whose honor meant more than his life.

The farmer's son would be out soon. First, he would milk Shelly the cow, and then he would put slop out for Charise the pig. The noisy chickens would be next. The chickens were the only group that Maury disliked. They weren't very smart and they did nothing but gossip all day long. Plus they seemed to always be underfoot, or under hoof, again depending on your perspective.

Rodney the duck would get old bread next. Then Maury would finally get his hay. He really thought he should be fed before those annoying chickens, but the farmer's son did not speak "horse," so all the naying in the world made no difference. After Maury, Bruce the goat got his grain and then Shelly got pushed out into the field.

The farmer's son would be in a bad mood by this time. Philo the dog would get some dry food after that, and then finally Kitty got her food. Kitty, of course, was a cat—pretty silly name for a cat, don't you think? The rest of the animals that visited the barn were expected to fend for themselves. After Barry, the next most popular outsider was Mike the mouse. He normally visited once Kitty left, but the barn had one standing rule, and that was no fighting, or stalking, each other in the barn.

Maury thought hard about those who frequent the barn, and no obvious suspect came to mind. Who after all would want to steal Charise's blue ribbon? It had no purpose other than sentimental value. It had been on the side of her stall for so long that most of the animals even forgot that it was there, but it really meant something to Charise. She cried most of the previous evening and Maury ran out of ideas on how to console her. It was the only thing she valued other than dinnertime.

Most of the animals were in attendance just before the farmer's son came out, as everyone was anticipating breakfast. Barry had just come in, so Maury thought it was a good time to ask some questions. He looked over his stall and loudly cleared his throat. Most everyone looked at him. "Has anyone seen Charise's blue ribbon?" All the animals within earshot nodded no. After a moment, Maury continued. "Have there been any strangers in the barn?"

The silence was broken by Mike the mouse. "I saw a couple of pigeons in here yesterday..."

Kitty was staring at Mike and it made him hide behind Philo. "I chased them out," replied Kitty as she licked her front left paw.

"Was anyone from the house in here yesterday? I mean, other than normal activity?" asked Maury.

Barry laughed. "What's normal for people? I've watched them my whole life, and they tend to do the strangest things. Have you ever seen them dress? I have never understood how their clothes always seem to fit them, and where do they come from?" asked Barry. The chickens all stopped in unison and stared at him with their mouth's open and blank looks on their faces. It was as if the question was more than their little brains could process. Then they noisily began to discuss this oddity among themselves.

"How do we know you didn't take it, Maury?" said Rodney the duck.

"Did you take it, Maury?" asked Mike the mouse.

"Nayyyy!" said Maury, and the animals laughed. They never got tired of that old joke.

"I bet Bruce took it!" said Shelly the cow. "Goats eat everything."

Maury looked at Bruce. "What about it, Bruce?"

The goat looked indignant, as if he had been insulted. "Everyone knows I didn't eat things that are blue!"

While the animals were talking, Barry studied the ground by the stall where the ribbon had been hanging. He thought he knew what had happened and how this would end. He wanted the culprit to confess, though, before the answer arrived. "I know this is hard for some of you….but the one who took it needs to come forward to repair his honor. We cannot have a liar or a thief in the barn. If we can't trust each other, who can we trust?" His short speech had no effect.

"Okay," said Maury. "I don't know for sure which one of you took it, but there will be a price to pay when we find out." Charise started crying again. Everyone looked sad, as it obviously meant a lot to her. Barry approached Philo the dog. "Don't you have something to say, Philo?" The dog's eyes widened and he put his head down.

"I'm sorry, Charise...I took your ribbon," confessed the dog.

Charise immediately stopped crying. "Where is it? What have you done with it?" she exclaimed. Philo was trying hard to remember. All he was sure about was that he chewed on it a little. He could not remember what he did with it. He knew she was going to start crying again. He was just about to answer when suddenly the barn door opened. Instantly everyone tried to act normal.

The farmer's son crossed the barn to Charise's small pen. He hung her blue ribbon back on the wall. He had cleaned it and pushed it back into shape. The one corner had bite marks on it, but Charise didn't care. It looked beautiful to her. The farmer's son smiled at the pig and then went over to milk Shelly. Once he was done, he went to the house with the milk, with all of the chickens following him out the door. Kitty ran out, too, followed by Philo. The dog stopped at the door and said, "Sorry, Charise...it won't happen again!" Then he ran off. Charise never heard a word as she stared at her ribbon. She was very happy now.

The dark-brown bay with the white spot in the middle of his forehead looked at Barry and said, "How did you know he took it?"

His friend smiled and said, "I could see where he scratched the side of the stall with his paws."

Maury nodded. "You know...I'm really glad to be your friend, Barry!" said the horse. "Thanks, Maury...I feel the same way!" The two animals smiled at each other. Maury shook his mane. "Plus, you're pretty smart for a rat!"

Barriers

I HAVE ALWAYS BEEN amazed by how much of our reality resides in our subconscious. So much of how we operate in society is dictated by guidelines that we have inside our heads and rarely do we thrust them out into the open. This story comes to be because of an event I experienced years ago that forced one such guideline of mine out into the light.

A number of years ago, I went into McDonald's with my children and ordered dinner. Because I ordered a simple meal, my food came out early. I went to a stretch of tables and sat facing the counters so I could watch my kids while they got their food. The seat I was on was a long plastic type of bench that ran for four sets of tables. As I sat down, I noticed a bus full of mentally handicapped children who were entering the restaurant with the intension of also "dining in." I will not judge this situation, but I will tell you that it was entertaining.

The first boy had his order filled while my four kids still waited at the counter for their "special orders," which left me eating french fries by myself at the stretch of tables. The young handicapped boy was, in my estimation, supposed to sit with his peers and the teachers who were overseeing the group. But because he was the first one with his order filled, he wasn't directed on where to sit.

Without the slightest hesitation, the young lad decided that he should sit with the only other customer in that section of tables. Now, I pride myself on being able to anticipate human nature and most of the time, I am prepared for the "strange" behaviors of people I do not know. But, I must confess, this young man raised the bar to a different level and I was caught off guard.

He crossed to the plastic bench and sat down, and then he put his bag and soda on the table. He then proceeded to slide down the bench, rapidly closing the distance on me. Frankly, I wasn't even thinking about him as I watched my children acting like part of the clientele that belonged on the bus. Suddenly I realized that "Little Mikey" was not only sitting next to me, but he is sitting with me.

Now, normally, people have "barriers." These barriers indicate where your personal space ends and where someone else's begins. When you talk to someone, you instinctively know how close you can get before you enter their "zone." And this barrier moves depending on what you're doing. When you play football, for instance, the barrier disappears completely, and when you are the guest speaker on a stage, the area increases significantly.

While eating at McDonald's, my estimated distance of comfort ability is about three people wide, unless you are one of my kids. "Little Mikey" was not one of my kids, and yet here he was. "How close was he? Let's just say he could not possibly have been any closer unless he was on my lap. His thigh and hip, his left shoulder and his elbow were adjoined to mine.

I looked to the right, and the young man was completely oblivious to the fact that he was committing a major breach of social etiquette. He was chowing down on his cheeseburger as if I wasn't even there. I stared at him and thought, *What the hell is happening?* And then I did something that I would not have anticipated. I started to laugh. The boy had no idea that it was the wrong thing to do, and I was so unprepared for the shock that I "tipped my hat" to his audacity.

I realized in that moment just how important these barriers are to us. They determine our comfort, our safety, our confidence, and even our mood. And yet this boy was totally oblivious to all of that. At first I was surprised, then I laughed at how ridicules it felt. But then I went into a different direction altogether—admiration. I actually envied him for his simplicity. He wasn't concerned with something that all of us sense, that all of us consider. I was thrust into a world where there was a possibility for limitless trust and ultimate comfort.

Not long after, "Little Mikey's" group assembled in another part of the restaurant and he was called away. Just then, my kids arrived at the table as he departed and said, "Who is he, Dad?" And I replied "Just some kid." At that moment, that boy *was* "just some kid." But now that I look back at it, he was much more than that to me. He was an instructor, a teacher, and an example to a man who had accepted "normal" for far too long without questioning the way we interrelate.

I get reminded of this event periodically by my female roommates. I own two young beagle sisters who also know of no boundaries. They sleep on each other and on guests and on me with no regard for barriers. They probably aren't really even aware of where they end and the other one begins. If it wasn't for the sensation of touch and feel, they probably would treat the other one's body as their own.

Obviously they are pretty different from "Little Mikey" of years past, but they do share a similar outlook on the world. They enjoy limitless trust and ultimate comfort. They are not concerned with whose space is whose unless there is food involved. They keep each other warm. They protect each other from the unknown. They even guard each other when one isn't feeling well.

When I lie down with them and they smash themselves up to me and fall asleep, I relax at a different level. And when I sleep with them and they are in the room, I trust their senses as if they were my own. My hearing, my eyesight, and my sense of smell don't really matter as much when they are around, because I rely on them. It is limitless trust. It is ultimate comfort.

I have been in a number of relationships, and never have I experienced the same kind of psychological ease that I do with my two pups. I am not saying I prefer dogs to women—honestly I am not, and I don't—but there is a deep lesson to be learned here. And it is independent to what I have enjoyed and experienced.

And what is this lesson? First, it is to understand where our barriers are and why. It is important to cognitively know why we set them where we do and think about whether or not it is appropriate or accurate. It should be something that we periodically do as part of our own self-inspection. I believe it can only improve how we interrelate with others.

And second, it is important to recognize what could be; that as a species, we have the potential to be closer to each other. That we can actually live in a world where our barriers aren't as large and aren't as immobile. That we can develop more trust and more comfort than we currently have and that we all can be more like "Little Mikey."

Choices

THE SUN WAS starting to set, and the spectators and the players were gradually making their way to the parking lot. Most of the cars that were there just minutes earlier were on their way out. It was just getting to the time where the only ones left at the baseball field were the stragglers and those cleaning up after the big game and the large crowd. With the departing people went the noise, the movement, and the controversy. It takes people to maintain drama; and when people disperse, so does the drama.

The dugouts were almost empty now. The visiting team was all packed up and had been swallowed up by a large yellow traveling party barge. The bus rocked with emotion as it slowly left the baseball field. The victors had stolen this game from the jaws of defeat leaving an angry, sad, and disappointed home team. The losers had a shorter trip home but they had to suffer through lectures and advice from over-zealous parents and friends who went through the "woulda-coulda-shoulda" playbook.

Coach Robinson was kneeling in the infield, removing third base from the ground and installing the "plug" to keep the dirt out. The events of the game continued to play through his mind as he tried hard to understand how his team let this one get away. The coach was a middle-aged former athlete who had been coaching this team for nine years. He was a good coach who won far more games than he lost. He had lost enough of the close ones to handle it okay, but this was a tough one. He knew when it was over that this was going to be one of those games that would define the season as "not quite good enough."

The coach stood up and dusted off his uniform. His next chore was to load up the equipment shed so he turned and began to carry the removed bases across the infield toward the small storage structure down the first base line. As he lumbered along, he noticed a lone figure sitting in the home dugout with his head down. He knew who it was and what was bothering him. He made a mental note to make that issue next in line on his "closing list" of things to do.

Jay sat on the bench with his head lowered. He was the shortstop on the baseball team and a senior and a team captain. Jay was a medium-sized kid who was thin, fairly quick, and always enthusiastic when it came to the game of baseball. This was his third and final year on this team, and he had hoped it would be a successful season.

Coach Robinson came up and sat on the bench a short distance away. He took some sunflower seeds out of his back pocket and began to chew on them. Jay looked up and his red face told a story that the veteran coach read right away. "So what's bothering you, Jay?" he asked.

Jay slowly raised his head again and said, "I hate losing. I know I threw that ball away...but Ben should have been at the bag. They never should have scored there. And then I struck out with the tying run on base. Now Ben is mad at me because I yelled at him...and we lost. I'm sorry, coach."

"Do you know why Ben wasn't there? When the batter dropped the bat to fake a bunt, Danny started to charge in at first, so Ben rotated toward first. Then when he pulled the bat head back and hit the groundball to you, Ben was too far away from second base to get there. It wasn't Ben's fault at all...it was Danny's. Danny isn't supposed to charge a bunt in that situation. Then you let the bad things in the top of the inning get you out of the proper mindset for you're at bat in the bottom of the inning," concluded the coach.

Jay hadn't realized why Ben wasn't there, and now it was as clear as day. "So that's why Ben yelled back at me. I'm gonna have to apologize later, aren't I, coach?" Jay watched as the sunflower seeds came back out of the pocket. "You know, Jay, I think you should call him right now." Jay nodded and took out his cell phone. Coach Robinson put away the scoreboard computer and locked the shed while the young man talked on the phone.

A little while later, Jay came walking toward him. He could tell by his posture that his spirits had improved. "Thanks, coach. I feel better. I wish we hadn't lost, though."

The coach turned to his shortstop. "You know, Jay, one thing the pros are very good at is getting their mind straight to perform. They take the last failure and tuck it away. They take a deep breath, clear their mind, and then start over."

The young shortstop nodded. "That is something I will have to get better at," he conceded.

Before he could walk away, the coach had one more thing to say. "You know, Jay, anyone can be a good winner. That's really pretty easy. But when things are the worst—and believe when I tell you that things can be far worse than losing a baseball game—but when things are their worst, that's when you find out who people really are." Jay nodded. "Somewhere, someday, boy, you'll have to figure out who you want to be." Jay nodded again even though he did not understand the reason for the short lecture.

"Well, I gotta go, coach. Me, Danny, and Ben are gonna go get ice cream!" The young man ran off to a car waiting for him in the parking lot. Coach Robinson wasn't sure if he understood or not, but talking to the young man actually made the coach feel better. And Jay seemed to be on the right path.

Three years later, Coach Robinson was having dinner when his phone rang. He stopped coaching two years earlier. When he answered the phone, he was surprised to hear Danny's voice on the other end. "Hey, coach. We're all here at Jay's going away party and we thought of you. We just wanted to say thanks for all you did for us." A tear welled up in the retired coach's eye as he asked, "Where is Jay going?"

"He joined the marines and he ships out to boot camp tomorrow."

When Coach Robinson hung up the phone, he realized how much he missed coaching the boys. He seemed to be unconsciously standing up straighter than normal as he was filled with pride that they thought enough of him to call. He also hoped that he had made a difference in the people they would become and the path that they would take. He thought back to the conversation that he and Jay had those three years earlier, and it suddenly hit him. "Maybe he was listening to me after all?"

Divine Intervention

THE ANT WALKED across the rocky hillside carrying a small leaf. His black body shimmered in the sun, and the little hairs on his abdomen glistened, but his beauty was not appreciated because there was no one there to see him. The insect was carrying a small succulent leaf in his mouth that was food for the colony. He had been struggling with his payload due to the wind and the slippery terrain, but his little mind was controlled by one simple thought, one simple assignment: return home with food.

Fatigue and pain were not considered in regard to the job at hand. He would complete his task or die trying. He would continue on with his mission no matter what the condition, obstacle, or inconvenience. His little mind was overwhelmed with thoughts of duty and direction. It was all that mattered to him.

The wind would blow, and the little creature would momentarily become airborne with his leaf. Then he would crash back to the ground, straighten himself, and return on the path to home. Sometimes he would hold his ground to the wind, sometimes all he could do was wait for it to put him back down. He was a veteran to these kinds of conditions as the days of being a pupa and a larva were far behind him.

The rest of the world tended to function in a larger arena, and his actions, his very struggle, would go unnoticed and unacknowledged by anyone who might appreciate it. This type of activity has been happening on earth with insects for millions of years. It is happening somewhere right now while you are reading this, and it will happen again tomorrow, somewhere, oblivious to all the other things going on in the world.

The ant continued forward with his cargo when suddenly a gust of wind stronger than the others caught him just right and lifted him off the path and tossed him toward the little stream that ran nearby. The little insect came down on the edge of an old dead leaf which hung directly over the running water. He clung there using every ounce of strength in his body. If he fell in the water, he would surely drown and his little life would extinguish unbeknownst to the rest of his colony, or for that matter, to every other living thing on the planet.

His concern in that instant in time was not for his own safety, put for securing his cargo that he held tightly in his mouth. He was close to failing and his body rejected and fought the thought of failure with every once of determination that had been programmed within him. His claws dug into the old dry leaf, and his body was stretched and extended to the limits that his frame was designed for. He was close to having his very limbs ripped out from his torso, but even that would have been acceptable if it meant accomplishing his mission.

The wind continued to blow, and the old dry leaf which he had anchored himself on turned over and threatened to fall into the stream. He began to lose his grip as he slid closer to the edge and closer to the water below. The dry leaf crumbled underneath his claws, and the wind and the weight of this predicament exceeded his grip. He now had no chance of moving forward. All he could do was delay the inevitable and postpone the event which every little brain cell in his head rejected. Every nerve in his body screamed in agony to a silent world that was unconcerned with such little things.

He instinctively pressed himself flat to the leaf to minimize wind resistance. It seems strange that he was capable of sensing the advantage of doing this even though his powers of reason have never been advanced enough to understanding why. It is like watching a horse standing in the shade of a lone tree on a hot summer day. He isn't capable of understanding the scientific explanations for thermal heat and radiation from

Sol, but he still makes the correct choice by avoiding the uncomfortable and intense solar rays.

This insect was almost to the end of the dry old leaf that kept him aloft. His will would not allow him to drop his cargo. He would take it with him into the water and to his death. If only his power of reasoning was advanced enough to consider an alternative. To drop his cargo would save his life, and then he could find more food. It seems simple to you or to me. But ants don't think that way and nothing short of divine intervention could save him.

The end was close now. One more gust of wind, and the struggle would end. The sun reflected off the water as it gurgled just below our stubborn arthropod. The mirror image underneath him went unnoticed. He might have thought it amusing to watch his reflection so close to destruction. There was no panic, no fear, no regret, only pain and duty. He hung on with one leg flapping in the breeze and then two. And then, suddenly, the angle of the sun miraculously changed and the old brown leaf turned over and came to rest back on the path that he had been following.

The little ant stepped off, landed on the ground, and scurried with his cargo toward the anthill and home. There was no thought given as to what just transpired. All he was capable of understanding was that another obstacle was gone, and reaching his goal and accomplishing his mission was now at hand.

An old man looked down at the insect as it triumphantly reached its nest. A certain satisfaction was found, not only by the insect but also by the man that had turned over the old brown leaf. Why did the old man intervene? It was the nature of the insect to follow his path, just as it was the nature of the old man to follow his. What path do you follow?

DO I BOW?

ANASTASIUS WAS BORN during the winter and took his place as part of a large family. He had nine brothers and sisters and they lived through a very poor childhood. As he grew up, his family did whatever it had to do to survive. They did every manner of work in the village, and all the children developed a great work ethic. Anastasius was the youngest, and he believed that is what motivated him to try as hard as he did.

Anastasius was average in size and weight and had no special features as a boy. In fact, he appeared so ordinary that few remembered his name. He became friends with the old blacksmith in town and was then lucky enough to be granted an apprenticeship at the smithy. Soon Anastasius was the best weapon designer around. He developed pride in his work and confidence in himself. People began to come from all around to his small town for his services. But this fame never went to his head and he stayed humble, but confident.

Then one day, a prince from the castle came to his smithy for a new sword. The prince had a reputation for being brutal and rude. As the prince entered the smithy, everyone bowed. Everyone, that is, but Anastasius. This infuriated the prince. He demanded that Anastasius acknowledge his superiority, but he would not give in. Anastasius was beaten severely and then exiled from the village and the surrounding lands.

Anastasius wandered for the next part of his life. He finally found a job teaching metallurgy at a large school many miles from where he began. He met a girl, got married, and became a father of a family of his own. He was a good husband and he spent many long nights teaching his children. He worked very hard during the day and loved his family dearly.

Anastasius' reputation as a knowledgeable instructor began to grow. Before long, the richest families would bring their children to learn from him. And then one day, a very wealthy aristocratic family arrived. They wanted to buy the school. They tolerated little and bought whatever they wanted, and when they entered the room, everyone bowed. Everyone, that is, except Anastasius. This angered the new owner of the school. Anastasius lost his job and was forced to leave town.

He and his family traveled far until they found a nice community by the sea. After a number of years, his children grew up and moved away. A few years later, his wife died from an illness and Anastasius was alone. He studied philosophy in his later years until he became a priest at the church. He would speak to crowds and his reputation grew. People would come from all over to hear his words.

Then one day, the archbishop came to town to meet this famous priest. The archbishop wore glamorous clothes and had many attendants. He was used to special treatment. He entered the church and crossed over to Anastasius. Everyone bowed—everyone, that is, but Anastasius. The archbishop was so incensed that he had Anastasius imprisoned.

Anastasius tried to live a peaceful life in his old age, but poverty and poor health made his remaining years difficult. He died on a winter day much like the one on which he was born. He left the world the same way he came in…alone.

Anastasius floated and drifted through a haze. Then suddenly there was a great light, and Anastasius had to squint to see. Then, as his eyes adjusted, he stood enveloped in a beauty his eyes had never seen before. He knew he was in the presence of the Almighty, and he was afraid.

God slowly lowered his head toward Anastasius but said nothing. Anastasius wasn't sure what to say, so he said the only thing he could think of: "Do you want me to bow?" God smiled and said nothing. Anastasius trembled in fear. Then in a deep and melodic whisper,

God said, "Do not be afraid, my son." Then God smiled and said, "Do you know what man stands before me?" Anastasius wasn't sure. He had been so many things. He shook his head no as he lowered his eyes. God reached out and grabbed his chin and held it up to his great, loving eyes. "It is the man who would not bow."

Emotion

ONE DAY, I woke up and stumbled into the bathroom. I turned on the bathroom light and made my way to the toothpaste. After fumbling about with groggy eyes and a saggy face, I finally managed to arm my toothbrush and began the process of removing the debris from an uneasy night of tossing and turning. As my eyes began to focus, a strange feeling came over me as I looked in the mirror. I realized that I did not recognize myself.

This odd sensation had less to do with looks and more to do with definition. I suddenly was asking myself: "Who am I?" This may seem trivial or senseless to those of you who are comfortable with your day-today activities, but I can assure you it wasn't trivial or senseless to me.

I began to answer the question from most important to least. I reaffirmed my Christianity, my fatherhood, my schooling, my athleticism, and my memory. But there is one aspect to my personality that I struggle with, and that is my emotion. I tend to be rather passionate with everything I do and everyone I know. This passion manifests itself in both positive and negative ways. There are times when I regret having a big mouth, but there are also times when I am proud that I spoke up. But even though my emotion is sometimes misplaced, I will never apologize for having it.

I have always believed that the display of passion is a thing of beauty, but I was never able to understand why I felt that way. I loved watching John McEnroe throw a fit. I was always captivated by Bobby Knight. Even watching Lucille Ball and her escapades fascinated me. It wasn't until I got into my late forties before I figured out why. When I connected the feeling with my religious beliefs, the answer shot out at me like a Nolan Ryan fastball.

In the Bible, John says that God is love (1John 4:8). I firmly believe that to be true. And what is love but a culmination of emotion? One might actually be able to make an argument that says "God is emotion." My first step in digesting this "revelation"(pun intended) was to compare what I believe emotion to be with what I thought God to be. So let me start defining some things that are all emotion.

Picture a cavalry rider charging into battle carrying the flag of his country or the flag of his unit. *The Charge of the Light Brigade* comes to mind here. Picture that trooper getting his horse shot out from under him. Now what does this poor soul do with his last living moment? He holds the flag up for somebody else to grab and to carry it forward. This is a pure and beautiful act of emotion, right to the death. Logic has absolutely nothing to do with it, but it unquestionably has to be done.

I can think of numerous examples of people who have functioned out of passion and have defied death itself. US Grant writing his memoirs with cancer, the men of the Second Continental Congress who signed the Declaration of Independence, and just about every Japanese soldier in World War II are just some examples.

Think for a second of every incredible feat of endurance, strength, or resilience and I will show you passion. Thomas Edison who would not give up, Abe Lincoln who functioned as president with an insane wife and a lost son, and Jackie Robinson who would not back down are good examples. When you take passion out of the person, they become very average indeed.

I have a pretty firm belief that deep passion is a significant thing, but where is the connection to God? I believe the connection is that passion overrides everything else. When an Olympic athlete competes on a broken leg, when a boxer fights on with a broken back, and when a ship's captain goes down with his ship, these are all examples of something so extraordinary—that a deeper power must be at work.

I think another connecting point comes straight from the stories in the Bible. God is always passionate. He challenges Moses and punishes those who digress. He challenges Abraham, too, with the near death of his son. He tests poor Job and he inspires John the Baptist, all done with emotion. Even Jesus unleashes his anger at the venders and gamblers in the temple. Yes, God is love, and I believe he is also emotion.

It is also important to point out that the things that separate humanity from the rest of the animal kingdom are also qualities that are founded in emotion—characteristics such as compassion, mercy, and honor, which are all based on emotion, and all of them get us closer to God.

I know what you're thinking; that when you see an annoying little kid who won't stop whining over something silly, or a wife crying because she chipped a nail, or an athlete wanting to fight over a perceived insult, those things are hardly evidence of a characteristic of God. And I would not consider those examples of advanced emotion. But wait until you see the spectacular achievements that some people make, things that leave you with your mouth hanging open, things that make you proud of your species, like how the people in New York responded to 9/11. That's when you will truly see my point. And you better not argue with me—I know I am right!

EMPATHY

HAVE YOU EVER wondered why a horror movie made back in 1940s just doesn't seem to be very scary? And then it makes you wonder if the people of that time were really scared by it when it was released. I could watch *Frankenstein* and its associated sequels over and over because they are entertaining, but I don't think of them as being very scary. Referring to them as "horror" movies seems inaccurate. And yet at the time of their release, they were perceived as being very scary. So my question is this: "What has changed in America?"

In order to answer this question, I will first expand on the symptoms that are related to the anomaly. For instance, the movies that I think are scary today probably would have killed people in the audience of the 1940s. There is no doubt that "special effects" are a monumental difference in movie design. But when I watch a drama, I find that some of the older movies were done as well as any movie today. I think as a culture our expectations of the "fantastic" in a movie are much higher than it used to be, whereas it is now common in a movie to see a guy ride a rocket, or single-handedly defeat an alien invasion. And yet if a movie was done well, regardless of the era, it will still captivate the audience.

I am still fascinated by such movies as *It's a Wonderful Life*, *12 Angry Men*, *The African Queen*, and *Midway*. The part of a movie I think is so affected by today's mentality is that big explosions are necessary now to captivate, whereas a good plot was the primary focus fifty years ago. But I think the universal truth with all movies, regardless of the era, is that we lack the necessary empathy to really appreciate the projected mindset.

To prove my point, how many times have you seen a murder or a death in a movie and think of it as only a plot point? But if you saw it in real life, you'd probably lose sleep for a month. Think of a war movie like *The Longest Day*. The retelling of the Normandy invasion of 1944 showed death on a massive scale, and yet I wasn't the least bit traumatized by watching it. I believe that is an indication that we have become "numb" as a society, at least in regard to how we view a movie. But I would go further and say we have also become "numb" in every other aspect of daily life.

Recently we had two news stories that ran in our local paper only a day or two apart from each other. The first story was about a young man who destroyed a small number of swan eggs in the town of Manlius. The swans have been a fixture in the pond there for years. The second story involved a middle-aged inner city man who was beaten, tortured, and left to die in a parking lot. Both of the stories received enough coverage to inform the local residents of the details. So having a brief introduction to these two events, which one do you think generated the most outrage and financial support for the victims? Well, it wasn't even close. The swan egg scandal involved a reward for information, an arrest, and large financial contribution from those concerned. There were also many more follow-up stories and a happy ending when new eggs were laid with a healthy offspring.

The other story about the inner city man who was beaten, tortured, and killed faded into obscurity right after the story ran. There was no outrage, no major police response, no fund raisers, and no arrests. Isn't it difficult to understand why the senseless murder of a human being should be so upstaged by a species of waterfowl? How did we get to a point in society where our children learn that "it's no big deal to kill an inner city man but nobody had better mess with our swan eggs!"

I contend that we are not capable of empathizing with the everyday tragedies of life, that we have become self-absorbed and selfish. It is obvious to me when I see people who are totally inconsiderate of others in regard to the simple interactions of the daily routine. I have personally experienced this in just about every aspect of living.

People today think it is okay to turn without signaling, to walk down the middle of a sidewalk and force you into the mud, to block a doorway leaving a full gym, to chitchat with the bank teller when there is a full line behind them, to smoke in a no-smoking area, to ignore your text message, to go in line at the grocery store that clearly says "seven items or less" when they have twelve things, and the list goes on and on. We as a society have lost the ability to consider each other, to think about the effects of our actions in regard to our neighbors, and we have become selfish and shallow.

We don't seem interested in empathizing with those around us. I don't think it is because we aren't capable; I think it is because the vast majority of people just don't care to. We have become isolated as a society and we have lost a large part of the fabric that used to bind us as a community. The block party, the social gatherings, a barn raising, the family get-togethers, the company picnics, dances, the chicken barbeque at the church, and the annual Christmas party are in danger of extinction. And with it, we lose an important part of the social fabric that used to hold us together.

I wonder how often the average person asks him- or herself: "I bet that person feels awful...I bet I would if I were him." I would guess that it isn't very often. We are indifferent and unconcerned about others as a culture. Very rarely do I notice a good deed, a polite act, courtesy above a business requirement, and a smile for no reason other than it looks like someone could use a good smile. And how can we teach our children about moral values and cultural norms if they only see them as a behavioral rarity?

The old adage about "leading by example" and the Christian principal of "treat others the way you would want to be treated" become more important now than ever. I have decided that I am going to change the way I go about living because of this. I have always bought lemonade from child proprietors whenever I see a stand. I had thought it was my meager way of encouraging youth and teaching them the ways of industry and the reward for putting in an effort. By now, my requirements have to be expanded to a new level.

My first duty will be to explain to my children what I see. I have to make sure that they are not a part of the problem and that they will join me in being part of the solution. I am going to make sure they practice empathy as often as I require it of myself.

My second duty will be to participate with my neighborhood, my workplace, and my friends. I have to lead by example and encourage others to do the same. This is not something I can profess and then do nothing to help it along. I will have to do more to make sure that all those good things about society don't disappear.

And the third thing I will do is to take the time to consider others more. I will be more aware of how others feel and determine what it is that I can do to help make it better. And then who knows? Maybe one day,

I'll watch the original *Frankenstein* again…and maybe this time, I'll understand why it was a "horror" film all those years ago.

Human Nature

IT WAS A cloudy day and the temperature was starting to drop. It started out as a comfortable morning, but now it was clearly cool enough to warrant a light jacket. The two figures sat on the steps and for the moment let the silence of the afternoon surround them. The man on the right was obviously starting to be bothered by the cold as he crossed his arms across his short-sleeved shirt. He would quickly rub his hands up and down on his forearms to offset the cool air that was descending down upon him. This was just one of the ways in which these two were different.

They sat on the steps that led up to the front door of Jameson's Iron Works. Both of them were employed inside, but the current day had concluded a short time ago. The two men were different in size, in color, and in the way they dressed. The only thing that seemed similar at that point in time was the blank look on their faces as they stared out across the street to the small park beyond.

The man on the right squinted as the sun momentarily poked through the clouds. He held his left arm out over his eyes to shield them while the figure on the left stayed completely motionless, oblivious to the temperature and the brightness of the afternoon. The discomfort of the direct sunlight awoke the man on the right from his confused state, and once again he tried to console his comrade.

"I think you should have gotten that promotion... Me personally, I think you were perfect for the job. You have the experience, you're a hard worker, you never miss a day...and you're as a strong as an ox."

The figure on the left barely moved. His lips parted briefly just long enough to mutter "Hhhmmmppfff!"

The man on the right continued. "But it wasn't up to me. They asked me what I thought. I told them you were the best choice...but they obviously didn't see it that way." Billy wanted to say more, but he didn't want to repeat himself. He believed in brevity, and his friend preferred that anyway.

Finally his friend broke from his apparent slumber in an attempt to understand his own dissatisfaction. "If what you say is true, then why didn't I get the promotion? You know I would do that job better than Peter. He makes way too many mistakes when he cuts." Billy nodded in agreement. "And he's lazy, but maybe they think his ability to deal with the other people in the shop was important." Quasi nodded. "You're saying he fits in better. I knew it was going to come to that."

Billy didn't want to bring up the topic because it was something he could not defend. Quasi turned to Billy. "It is my color...the fact that I don't look like everyone else...that I wasn't born here...that's what it really is... isn't it?" Billy stared straight ahead. He didn't want to say it, but he knew it was true. Even he felt uncomfortable sometimes. Not because he didn't like his friend, but sometimes his coworkers would look at him funny because they were friends.

"I've tried to understand this myself," said Billy. "It's human nature. People are afraid of things and people that are different or uncommon. They function best when they are comfortable...when they are not worrying about other things."

Quasi turned and looked out across the park. "But I've lived here for six years now. I know everyone in there. This is my home, too, Billy...I will always be different than them. Does this mean that I have to accept being a second-class citizen because I don't speak English as well as them, or because I look different than they do?"

Billy was ashamed. He knew his friend's heart. He trusted him. He believed in him. And yet he knew he could not fix this. "I'm sorry, Quasi...it might take a very long time before they can accept this. It's a small town...kind of a 'cornbread town'..." he trailed off. After six years, it should have gotten better, but it hasn't. In some ways it has gotten worse. Billy knew it was because Quasi made them look bad.

Billy wanted to say something profound, but all that came out of his mouth was "Its human nature." Quasi went back to looking like a statue while Billy once again began to rub his arms. "At least you have one friend," concluded Billy as he, too, stared across the street at the park.

Billy wished he had brought a jacket. The thought of a coat never crossed Quasi's mind. You see, robots don't get cold.

I Dream of Jeanne

ARLIN WALKED ALONG the beach as the waves washed up on the shore. The sand was strewn with small rocks and shells, but he still managed to navigate a path through them. The sky was cloudy and dark. He expected it to rain before he got back, but he didn't mind. He actually preferred to get wet. It would match his state of mind.

Arlin had relegated himself to living a lonely life. The girl that he loved had passed away at about this time two years ago. He blamed himself for her death, but the reality was her death could not have been prevented whether he was there or not. But no one could convince him otherwise.

He found it difficult to perform his daily duties until he settled his mind, so he would walk the beach early in the morning before he started his day. This helped, but it wasn't a cure. He was constantly told to move on and to get on with his life, but he did not know how.

Arlin had a good life, but without his love, he found it impossible to enjoy it. He often wished his father was still alive; he would know how to help him. His father died many years ago. They were very close and this, too, was difficult for Arlin. He still remembered some of the lessons he learned. "Always be a gentleman," his father would say, "until you have a very good reason not to." "Only weak men lie!" was one that he heard often. Another saying he loved to recite was, "Any adversary can be bested; you just have to know his weakness and exploit it." Arlin very rarely had to apply any of this advice. His father had given him directions that seemed to have a way of dealing with everything in life—everything, that is, except for a lost love.

Arlin had started out earlier than normal this morning so he decided to temporarily veer off the beach. The demon cave was unusually loud. *It probably had something to do with the wind direction,* he thought. So he decided to experience the full effect. The cave was large and dark, and few people ever ventured inside. It was rumored to be the home of an evil spirit, hence its name. Arlin never believed in any of those stories and so he turned inside. He had been in this spot dozens of times but never went in very far. He felt it was best to leave the "demon" alone, just in case he really was inside.

He stood in the opening of the large cave as the wind howled past him. The ocean had a way of turning this whole side of the hill into one big musical instrument. "That's probably where the idea of a demon comes from," he concluded. He had his fill of the effect and was about to turn away when out of the corner of his eye he saw something odd. There was just enough light to see what looked like a small box sticking out of the ground inside the cave. It appeared to be partially buried under a large, flat rock and mostly covered with sand. Arlin decided to go in and get a closer look. The box appeared to be very old and it had a strange writing on its lid. A small clasp on the lid kept the top down.

Arlin picked up the box and shook it. He could feel something inside the box rolling back and forth. It was heavy for its size. He studied the writing for an instant but none of it had any meaning to him. Before he thought it through, he undid the clasp and opened the box. The cave was suddenly filled with a bright-red light, and as it dimmed, he saw through his squinting eyes an apparition of incredible size solidifying right before him. Arlin was so startled that he dropped the box.

Orthazar was close to eight feet tall, bright red, and had a tail. He looked down at the surprised young man with disdain. "Pick up my box, toad!" he bellowed. "Who are you to enter my cave?" Arlin kept his eyes to the ground. "I'm no one of consequence, great lord." Arlin knew right away that the demon thought very much of himself. He instinctively decided to try to act in the way the demon perceived him. He briefly considered if this was something learned from one of his father's lessons.

"Why have you trespassed here?" bellowed Orthazar.

"Ignorance, lord...I did not know this was your cave," answered Arlin quickly.

"You are either a liar or a great fool. Either way, I don't like you." He waved his hand, and in a flash of bright-red light, Arlin suddenly found himself imprisoned in Orthazar's box.

"Keep my box warm, toad, while I enjoy my freedom." Orthazar set the box down on the large, flat rock. Then he laughed loudly and prepared to walk away.

Arlin knew he had to think quickly. "As you command, lord! It is too bad that you will miss the arrogant king, though, but I will abide."

Orthazar had taken two steps toward freedom but paused at Arlin's response. "What king?" demanded Orthazar.

Arlin realized he only had one chance at this. "The king of Orin? He is the one who ordered me to inspect your cave. He intends to vanquish you to appease the local town's people. I was sent to find out if you really did reside within. I suspect the king really isn't as brave as he pretends to be."

Orthazar stepped back toward the box. "And why would you tell me of this? A trick, I suppose, to save yourself?"

"No, great lord. I have little to live for. It would be nice to see justice though," responded Arlin.

Orthazar became came curious. "You would betray your king?"

"He is not my king, great lord. He is responsible for my lost love, and I would enjoy nothing more than to see a bad king suffer!"

Orthazar rubbed his hands together. The idea of besting a king was more than he could turn away. "Would you send this king to me?"

"I believe your intension would be to humble a bad king. And I am all for that. If given the opportunity, I would promise that you would meet this king before the sun sets this day."

Orthazar was convinced the "toad" was telling the truth. "Very well," said Orthazar. "But if you have any thoughts of betraying me, I will make you suffer beyond what you can imagine!" And after another flash of bright-red light, Arlin was standing next to the demon. "I will go back into my box. Bring this king to me, and you will have your justice!"

Arlin smiled. "I swear you will meet him this day."

Then with another burst of bright-red light, Orthazar disappeared back inside his box. Arlin picked it up and pushed the clasp down, sealing it closed. He looked at the writing again and realized it must be a curse that keeps the demon trapped within. A look of profound sadness crossed his face as he thought of his lost love. "What do you know about suffering?" he muttered.

Arlin took the box and buried it at the base of the large, flat rock where he found it. He made sure it was deep enough that no one would accidentally stumble upon it. He smoothed the ground to conceal the place it was buried. Then he walked out of the cave and continued down along the beach. He realized his father's advice had saved him.

Arlin wondered if there would ever be a need to revisit that box. *Maybe someday*, he thought. The future was uncertain. He had a lot to worry about as his kingdom had many challenges that he needed to overcome. He hoped to be just as great a king as his father had been. He smiled as he walked around the shells and rocks on the beach. He only told Orthazar the truth. He had met the king this day.

I Wonder

I HAVE ALWAYS BEEN interested in the perception surrounding people who make predictions. Everything from gambling to fortune telling, from global warming to horoscopes, and from the stock market to the weather forecast is nothing more than somebody trying to convince me of something that is going to happen. And there are a significant number of people who will be sold on someone else's opinion, and I suppose that is the reason that these topics are so prevalent in the news.

Some of these predictions are based on a significant amount of data and research, and other things have no foundation to stand on, and yet people listen anyway. And if someone is ever correct about a prediction, they become regarded as some brilliant mind who can see more than anyone else. Jeane Dixon, Jimmy the Greek, and Joe Namath are some examples of this phenomenon. The list that someone could make of people who were right about a rare prediction would probably fill a phone book. But does someone's success in the past guarantee that they will be correct in the future? Of course it doesn't.

Personally, I think that there are vast examples from history of things that can happen and are destined to repeat themselves. The question really isn't "if" but "when." Big earthquakes, volcanoes, hurricanes, or asteroid strikes are all potential disasters looming to repeat themselves. And yet there are other forecasted topics which just become silly. I remember when Ted Danson predicted that if we did not stop polluting the ocean, all of humanity would be dead in ten years. Or how about the outlandish Mayan calendar forecast? And what will the world say about them in 2013 when the date has come and gone? It will also show how many foolish people bought into it.

Of course, natural calamities are out of our control...but what about the things that are "in our control"? Those man-made disasters which are looming—terrible things born from overpopulation, genetic interference, reliance on automation, and our general and complete betrayal of mother earth. Our control over these things is an illusion. There are so many bad possibilities…but let's not forget about our worst bad habit—war.

War on a world scale is inevitable—it is inevitable—but when? I suspect it is closer now than most people can foresee. And how bad will the next one be? I shudder to think about it. But it is a strange thought indeed to think that I might wake up one morning to no cell phone, to no electricity, and to death on an unimaginable scale. But how can anyone predict "when"? It might not happen for two hundred years…or a thousand…or it might start tomorrow.

The end of the world is, I think, the most predicted unscientific topic ever discussed. People have been doing it for thousands of years. Everyone and every prediction up until now has been wrong—every source—from Nostradamus to Harold Camping. It says in Matthew (24:36) that no one will know the day except God.

I have a deep confidence in humanity. But there are so many variables, so many possibilities, so many contributing factors, so many unseen or unrealized dangers that could lead to our destruction…and then there are those random individuals who somehow get into levels of power when they should never have been allowed to get that close. Stalin, Hitler and Pol Pot come to mind.

If the end comes, will it be a big ball of flame that eradicates everything quickly and mercifully? Or will it be a slow, lingering trauma where we rotate in the depths of hell with no hope of salvation? And how will we react to these events? Will we turn on our brothers and sisters? Or will we stick together and show our true colors, like 9/11 at the World Trade Center? Or maybe it won't happen at all? Maybe I am just as guilty in my visions as all of those who predicted "doomsday." But I will conclude these random thoughts with a short description that I refer to as "I wonder."

I wonder if a day is coming when everything that we expect in life will end—when war and famine and disease will destroy the very fabric that once held everything together. And if that day comes in our lifetime, you'll learn who your friends really are, and who it is you can really trust and really believe in. Those phony masks born from fat comfort and fat lifestyles will melt away and will be replaced by brutal and violent life choices. People will have their perceptions of humanity and righteousness ripped out from under them like the French Revolution. And then it will be clear to those who never saw it coming. And they will ask, "How did we ever let it come to this? How could we have been so stupid?"

On that day, our true nature will undress and show through for all to see, naked in view to those who thought they knew us. In that moment of time, we will live the judgment day, and the only thing that will prevent us from becoming animals will be the inner light that some of us cannot betray no matter what happens. Maybe on that day, I will be able to show the world what it is about me that separates who I am from other men, and then everyone will know. And they will say, "So that is who he is!" I pray for all of this to be wrong. And if it is wrong and it doesn't happen, I hope I die before I end up in a nursing home. I require a quick death—a meaningful one—to die with a purpose; I beg the Lord for this. But either way, I'm playing golf on Friday, and I will worry about the end of the world some other time.

Inner Pain

A FLY LANDED ON the bar. It stood motionless for a full two seconds. This is probably equivalent to you or me sleeping for two days. Then it turned its body to the left. It appeared to move so quickly that to the naked eye it wasn't clear whether or not it hopped or took deliberate steps. It put its head down and began to suck on the bar. It had to have been attracted to some leftover grease from a lunch long past. Then it flew off to share the afternoon with some other patron.

Green eyes stared at a glass of beer. No words were spoken. There was condensation on the sides of the glass that would gather into a droplet and then would tumble and run in an erratic path to the bottom until its fate was consumed by the cardboard coaster lying underneath. The beer within had been cold but was now starting to lose its intended temperature. The heat of the afternoon speeded up this process without any regard to the pleasure of those in attendance.

Suddenly the silence was broken by a large, old, fat man. He was clean-shaven, and his attire indicated he was trying hard to improve his appearance. He crossed the room and sat down on the bar stool next to the spot where the beer was slowly getting warmer. There wasn't quite as much in the glass now as there was when the fly took his leave, but it was still more full than it was empty. No words were spoken as the large, old, fat man motioned for the bartender's attention.

The young lady behind the bar but a coaster down in front of him and said, "Hi Dave. Blue Light?"

He put on a sly smile and nodded. "Hi, Brittany. How was your birthday?" Then she went on a three-minute rant of events and acquaintances. The large, old, fat man acted as if he cared. Green eyes momentarily looked at the intensity of his conversation and instantly became revolted by the implications.

The large, old, fat man, who obviously suffered from loneliness, was as about as delusional as a poor man buying a mega-millions lottery ticket. Brittany reached forward with her cell phone to expose a large tattoo on her arm than ran from her wrist to her elbow. Its pattern and design held some meaning, but it really meant very little to the viewer. She showed the large, old, fat man a picture that was stored on the device.

"Is that you?" he inquired. The bartender then went into another long diatribe of her weekend adventure. The view on the other side of the bar was more interesting. Nothing was happening over there. There were two young men sitting at a small table. They were obviously reenacting a confrontation that had happened the day before. It was either a combination of events involving darts and alcohol or bowling and alcohol. Either way, it really didn't matter.

The two young men both wore baseball caps. Both of them wore them backward. It must also be some sort of fashion statement. Was it intended to give the appearance of a rebel's attire? Were these two the modern-day gunslingers who now frequent saloons in the twenty-first century? Three years ago it was flat brims. Three years before that it was curved brims. Three years from now it will be some other distortion of the baseball cap.

Behind the bar was a large mirror. Initially it was believed that it was a simpler and less complicated direction to stare, but that was quickly dispelled as the image that filled the looking glass was anything but simple. It showed a phony aura of phony people in a phony room. It also showed a quarter glass of beer rapidly getting warmer. It exposed a tramp stamp on a twenty-five-year-old bartender who was trying to get a good tip from a large, old, fat man who thought he had a chance. It uncovered two high school dropouts whose biggest adventure in life was to embarrass some other high school dropout on a Friday night. And it revealed lines of sadness and pain borne from the miscalculation of a relationship that had spun out of control.

Brittany saw that the beer glass was now empty and without asking went to the cooler and pulled out a new one. She filled the new glass close to the top while the large, old, fat man continued to inquire about her weekend. She had calculated that she had spent more than enough time talking about herself to keep him happy for a while. She removed the old glass and set the new cold glass of beer in front of grateful green eyes.

"Thanks."

"You're welcome."

Memories of how it all unfolded came flooding back into the forefront of the mind. Words were spoken that were harsh and cruel. Facial expressions and body gestures were recalled, and explanations that made no sense were replayed again. The truth will never be uncovered. There were suspicions and accusations—none of which were based on fact, most of which were pieced together by clues and hints that very well might have no meaning whatsoever.

People love to speak in consoling phrases whenever possible. "God never gives you more than you can handle," "Things happen for a reason," "God never closes a door without opening a window," and so on and so forth. In all reality, they sound good, and I guess you can grab whichever one makes you feel better. I suspect that reality has a different meaning altogether, and satisfying perception really doesn't change who you are, where you are, or where you will end up.

The bartender walks to the far side of the bar to greet two regulars who have just sat down. The mirror now shows that the large, old, fat man reacts by sitting quietly. He now has a dejected look as he gives his full attention to his bottle of Blue Light. The two young men who were wearing the ball caps on backward have gotten up to leave, and the lines of sadness and pain still continue to reflect in the mirror.

A fly lands next to the beer glass just as another drop of condensation rolls down the side of the half-filled glass. Could it be the same insect? Or is it a family member inspecting terrain previously investigated by a distant relative? The fly moves in a zigzag motion just as the drop of water disappears into the coaster. It hesitates and is completely motionless for a full two seconds. Then it flies off and leaves the half-filled glass of beer and the green eyes staring into the mirror.

It Was Close...

SATCHEL STOOD IN the ring waiting for his sparring partner to get his headgear on. He took on his normal "ring persona" by dancing while he waited. His short skips and bouncing seemed almost as if he was doing it to music, but everyone in the room knew that you don't get to be the number one middleweight contender in the state without being all business in the ring. Satchel pounded his gloves together once his training opponent was ready, and then they began. Satchel worked on his form, quickness, and different combinations that he had planned. He only had one week left before his big fight, and he was almost ready.

His manager stood by the ring and watched. Tony studied his approach and technique and made mental notes to discuss with his fighter later. This session lasted thirty minutes and then Satchel spit his mouthpiece into the water bucket. His body glistened with sweat as he climbed out of the ring. He would shower, change, and then meet with Tony and Barney, his trainer, before calling it a day. Most of these meetings involved watching video footage and discussing the progress toward the next fight.

Satchel entered the video room and sat at the table. It was strange to him that the TV console was still parked up against the far wall. A few moments later, Tony came in and sat down across from the young fighter. "Satch, I think it is time to consider what it is you want out of life."

Satchel's forehead crinkled and he asked, "What do you mean?"

Tony pushed his folder off to the side, giving a clear indication that this discussion was based on emotion and not based on statistics.

"I've been noticing that you have been spending a lot of your free time with Melissa..."

Satchel frowned. "Yeah...so what?"

Tony knew Satchel wouldn't like this conversation. "This is a distraction you cannot afford. I believe it is hurting your chances in this next fight—that you are behind in your training—and worse yet, you are not focused with the job at hand." Satchel did not respond so Tony continued. "You are going to have to decide if you want to make a career out of boxing...or not."

It was the first time Satchel had ever had a disagreement with Tony. He felt awful. He looked up to him like a father. But things were even more complicated now because he realized that he was falling in love with Melissa, and turning her away was just not going to happen. He tried to make the case that she makes him a better fighter. He pointed out that Melissa motivates him, but Tony wasn't buying it. Tony countered by saying that unless he could give him some "proof" that the relationship had a "plus" side to it, he would have to insist that they cool the relationship, or he would have to walk away from his favorite fighter.

Satchel walked the streets for an hour once he left the gym. *Could Tony be right?* he thought. There had to be an advantage to his relationship with Melissa that made him a better fighter. There had to be something that he could show to his manager to prove it. But as hard as he tried, nothing came to mind.

He finally showed up at Melissa's apartment for dinner. Her face was red, and he knew that she had been crying. "Sorry, I'm late," he said. "Our meeting ran long." She did not look up. "Why didn't you call?" she said with a sniffle. The sniffle was so slight that he only heard it because he was so focused. Ordinarily he would miss something like that. He was always looked at as a brawler by the people who knew him. Melissa was making him see things he had never noticed before. He suddenly decided to come clean with the truth.

What are you going to do, Satch?" she asked. He did not know the answer.

The night of the championship fight came. His opponent was Big Ben Taylor (who wasn't really very big), an undefeated champion. Ben was solid muscle and very fast. Satchel was a two-to-one underdog. Ben was in line to move up nationally in the middleweight division, and a lot of people thought he had the chance to win the world belt. If Satchel was going to go anywhere, tonight was the night to show it.

Big Ben had sixteen fights and sixteen knockouts. Two of them were TKOs, but no one went the distance against BB Taylor. Satchel not only intended on going all the way, he intended to win. When they stood in the center of the ring before the fight, Satchel knew he had his work cut out for him. The magnitude of this challenge landed on him like a crushing right hand to the jaw.

The bell sounded, and Barney encouraged him to match BB Taylor. Tony, his manager, had not talked to him for a week. Satchel was focused nevertheless, and the two men traded punches. The first round was just about even, and Satchel soon realized how strong his opponent was. He showed no emotion and fought like a machine. As he sat in his stool while his trainer wiped his forehead, he noticed Barney had his laptop open to the Vegas gambling site. "What are the odds on me?" he asked. "Two to one against" said little Tommy, Barney's helper.

Satchel went out for round two and took two solid punches to his face. He was cut below his left eye. His legs were still strong but he knew he had lost this round. He figured he would be down two to zero now as draws almost always go to the favorite. The bell rang, ending the round, and Satchel went back to his stool. Barney worked on the cut while Satchel caught his breadth.

"Stay with the plan, Satch...and for the love of God, win this next round" said Barney.

As Satchel prepared for the third round to start, little Tom blurted out, "Three to one now." The bell rang and Satchel went to work.

Satchel had one good left hook to the chin but it seemed to do no damage to BB Taylor, the machine. He wasn't even fazed and that disappointed the challenger. But he did win the round. He knew he still had a chance.

After seven rounds, Satchel was starting to get tired. He knew he was either down five to two or four to three, depending on the scorers. BB Taylor seemed as fresh now as he had at the start. Satchel was starting to doubt his own ability. He wondered how he could last for twelve rounds against this guy...and win. He waited for the bell to ring, and little Tommy whispered, "five to one."

In round nine, Satchel was a mess. His nose was bleeding and was probably broken. The cut under his eye was worse, and the referee told his trainer that "It was close..." Satchel knew he had to do something, but he didn't know what "it" was. It was starting to look like Tony was right. BB Taylor still looked the same and just as fresh. Satchel thought, *he has to be tired... he has to be.*

Round ten started, and Satchel took two combinations that made him stagger. BB tried to put him away but the bell sounded. Satchel trotted back to his stool, and the small crowd was disappointed that the knockout blow was avoided. Satchel enjoyed the cool water on his face. He thought of how upset Melissa was when he came in late a week ago. He remembered that little sniffle. Then the bell went off and round eleven began. The last thing he heard was little Tommy yelling "twelve to one."

Satchel's strength was gone. BB Taylor was now hitting him significantly harder than what he could repay, but he did his best to avoid the big blow. Satchel threw a left jab to his ribs after BB missed with the right. It seemed harmless enough, but through swollen and bloody eyes he saw something. BB winced as he pulled back his right arm. The facade of invincibility came crashing down. Satchel suddenly decided to make one last effort to win this fight. He threw everything that he had remaining into a barrage that pounded BB's right side. The fighter was obviously in much more pain than anyone knew.

Soon the defense cracked as BB could not lift his right arm to defend himself. He tried to clench Satchel to last out the round but the challenger would have none of it. A hard straight left found its way into BB's right cheek and the undefeated champion collapsed to the floor. He lay there in a daze right up to and past the standard ten count. Satchel had won.

Later he confronted Tony. "You know…if it hadn't been for Melissa, I don't think I would have noticed that he was hurting far more than he led on…"

Tony smiled. "Okay, son. You were right. We will go forward from here."

The press came in and wanted a quote for their stories. "Champ! Champ! Did you think you were going to lose?" they hollered.

Satchel smiled. "It was close…"

It's Just the Train, Rueben

RUEBEN TRIED TO stay awake, but between his lack of sleep and the warm sunlight, he found himself drifting off. He sat on the wooden bench in the crowded train station by himself with his arms and legs crossed in front of him. His white hair hung down slightly over his face as his head drooped. His short white beard compressed on his chest as his chin lowered. His clothes were slightly wrinkled but clean. To a passerby, he had all the appearance of a man who had been traveling for a while. Rueben was not concerned with how he looked as his eyes closed. The twinkle from the sunlight that had been reflecting off his eyes was now gone.

"Hey, Rube? Are you coming?" she said. The girl in the light-blue dress stood by the car door with her left hand on her hip. She jokingly tapped her right foot in an attempt to show her date they she was being made to wait. The smile on her face ran from ear to ear as the young man desperately tried to fix his zipper. The tux he wore made him uncomfortable. It fit him all right, but its design and complexity was more than he had control over. He was doing his best to gracefully conceal his actions, but his face took on a red shade nevertheless. He spun to trot to the car and stumbled over a crack in the sidewalk. He disliked looking clumsy but he knew that would be his fate tonight.

Dating Catherine was a dream come true. He was nervous. She was such a pretty girl, and every boy in the class wanted to date her. He wasn't really sure why she said yes when he asked her to the prom, but he was going to try hard to make it memorable. He stood at the driver's door as his parents stared at him from the front porch. The camera still hung from his mother's left hand as she waved to her son. He took a deep breath and got in the car. He suddenly realized that he knew very little about the girl sitting next to him.

The momentary silence was broken by a child carrying a large stuffed bear. Her heels made a clicking noise on the hard floor as she skipped by Rueben as he slept. The sound disrupted his breathing long enough for him to recover by blasting out a sigh. His chin rose slightly as if he was going to awaken, but then it settled back down to his chest and he resumed his previous posture.

Randy was a big kid as he stood at almost six feet six inches tall. Rueben thought of him as a kid even though they were both twenty-three years old now. "Rube, why do you want to marry her? I don't see how you could trust her? This is going to be the biggest mistake of your life. You are going to pay for this for years!" Rueben looked at his friend but said nothing. A short smile began to creep across his face, and Randy knew it meant he wasn't going to heed his advice. "Okay, fine. Go ahead and ruin your life. Just remember later on that I told you so!" The big kid with the blond hair tossed his napkin at him. Rueben swayed to the left as the crumpled piece of cloth bounced off the cushion of the chair next to him.

The waitress stopped at their table. She refilled both of their soda glasses and then she moved on to the next set of customers. "So, the issue is trust?" asked Rueben.

Randy began to lean back in his chair like he was an expert. "Of course it's about trust—everything is about trust. Without trust, what have you got with anybody? Nothing." Rueben stared at him as his mind raced. Randy tried to drive home the point. "Who can you trust? I mean really trust." At first Rueben thought it was funny. He started considering a number of people in his head. He had to eliminate "kind-of-trust." Then "trust" was crossed off, and he was left with "really trust"—since his father died last year, just his mother. Rueben had no idea at the time, but he would remember that conversation his entire life.

A family walked by the bench and a little girl was crying. "I want to stay home with Stacy," she hollered. Her mother angrily pulled her by the arm toward the ticket window. Rueben took a deep breath but did not awaken. Instead he blew out a heavy exhale that made his beard wiggle slightly, and then he was motionless once again.

"Mr. Sizemore? Mr. Sizemore?"

"Yes?" said Rueben. He didn't like the sound of his last name being used by the doctor.

"I'm sorry, sir...but your mother has passed on." Rueben knew it was time. She had fought for so long. He secretly hoped it would end because the frail, unconscious woman really wasn't his mother anymore. Tears welled up in his eyes. "I'm really, sorry young man," said the old doctor as he put his hand on Rueben's shoulder.

About a month later, Rueben finally realized his mother was truly gone. He completely understood the significance of the change now. His one "ace in the hole," his one unquestionable ally, the one person that he had left in the world whom he could really trust, no matter what, was gone. This time he cried hard. He wept in the shower and he let the water wash away the tears as fast as they appeared on his face. He realized the world would be a different place now.

Suddenly his mind raced forward to the day that Randy died. He had been his friend for forty years. Then time shot backward and he once again remembered the day they talked about trust. Then his memory raced forward, and he relived how they let him down at work years later. The memory of his sister taking all of the things that belonged to his recently deceased mother came back to him as well. He remembered the sting of his so-called friends at the bowling alley replacing him without even so much as a phone call. This was your life, Rueben!

"Randy? Randy?" he blurted out. "Are you there?" He was in a deep, restless sleep now. He began to turn back and forth on the bench. "I'm sorry, Randy! I'm really sorry…I should have been there!" he mumbled. A few of the people who passed by the bench looked in his direction as they walked around him, but no one stopped. The old man in the wrinkled clothes with the short white beard seemed like he belonged on that bench, that somehow, that is right where he was supposed to be—at that place and time—and that he should not be disturbed. And even though his body trembled and shook in the middle of this nightmare, no one intervened.

At that instant in time, as the world suddenly slowed and finally froze in the middle of his dream, a flood of regret washed through him like a strong wind pushing through a grove of trees. The appearance of his face changed from one of fear to one of deep sadness. It was as if his face was trying to show the world how an old man can contort himself to make his scars and experiences look like a work of art.

Suddenly Randy's face was there, and he pointed at his longtime friend. "Who can you trust, Rube? Who can you really trust?" And then in a loud screech, the locomotive that approached the platform pulled on its brakes and the vibration and sound from this iron horse could be heard all across the station. Rueben popped up with a start with beads of sweat on his forehead. He sat up straight with a confused look that yelled out "What's happening? Where am I?"

In that instant, his eyes slowly focused on the old woman in front of him. She stood there with two cups of coffee held out in front of her. She had a smile on her face that ran from ear to ear as she reached one cup across to him. He had known that smile for fifty years. He reached out for the coffee as she said, "It's just the train, Rueben." His face changed from one of desperation to one of relief. *Who do I trust, Randy?* he thought. *I trust her.*

Just a Coincidence

THERE ARE MANY aspects to existing that become hard to understand. Two people can look at a common event and come up with two completely different interpretations of why it unfolded the way that it did. How is it possible for this to happen? Maybe we lack faith, or maybe it is that we lack confidence with our own understanding of reality? Some people easily see the fantastic. Other people wouldn't see that perspective if a bona fide leprechaun handed them a pot of gold from the bottom of a rainbow. And most of us occupy the different levels in between these two extremes.

One thing is certain with all of us though. There comes a time when our confidence wanes and we start to doubt what it is we are experiencing. And then, when it becomes more than what we can explain away, we come to the conclusion that we just experienced something fantastic. Think of what I am attempting to convey by considering one of the most common explanations for confused reality: the ghost sighting.

A ghost sighting is something most of us can attest to either experiencing firsthand at one time in our lives or by repeating a rather passionate retelling of someone else's experience with the supernatural. Sometimes it is retold by stating, "I'm not sure if I believe that story, but the person who told me—they believe it!"

Now think about the steps that lead to this type of interpretation. The first thing that happens is that one of our senses becomes aware of a something out of the ordinary. It could be a sound, a sight, a sensation, a smell, or even a taste. We then try to put an explanation to that sensation. We draw from our vast memory of experiences for these types of conditions. When we cannot match an explanation to the experience, we tend to investigate to understand what it is that we are "missing." For example, *What is that sound? It kind of sounds like water dripping. I'll just go into the bathroom and see what that is... Oh, someone used the sink and didn't turn the faucet completely off. I'll just turn that knob... there! Another mystery solved!*

But what happens when our further investigation does not yield a reasonable explanation? We begin to consider a wider and more fantastic array of possible explanations. This divergence from reality varies in velocity based on the individual. Some people drift very quickly. Others stubbornly refuse to accept the fantastic as a possible explanation no matter what.

The people who drift very quickly, they get labeled as "whack jobs"; and the people who refuse to drift, they get labeled as "hardheads." How safe it is for the rest of us to be neatly nestled in the middle, between these two perspectives. And we employ our own personal standards to explain away all of life's unexplained mysteries—everything from angels to fairies. Think about this for a second. Every fantastic explanation that is a response to the unknown—it is concocted to explain the unexplainable. Everything from gremlins, werewolves, ogres, witches, goblins, ghosts to trolls, dragons, elves, wizards, pixies, and vampires. I'm sure you could probably name thirty more by putting a little thought into it. The list grows even larger if you incorporate other cultures, both past and present. So why does humanity have such a long list of the fantastic? Is it because of what we don't know? Or is it because we enjoy creating a mystery to entertain? Maybe it is a combination of both?

I think so far, most of you can relate to what I have presented and would not disagree to my description. But now, I am going to take the same tendency toward the fantastic, and turn it to discuss a different perspective on life. I will start by saying that I believe people are creatures of habit. The way that most people respond to one set of conditions is similar to the way that most people would respond to an equally confusing aspect of life. My conclusion at the end is probably not going to be what you would expect, however.

Think about the last time you experienced a coincidence. Did you attribute a meaning to it? Or did you just make note of it and let it go? What about the last time you had a really weird instance? Let's just say you mentioned a dream you had about your mother, then you heard her first name mentioned on the radio and, at that precise moment, you knocked her picture over on your desk? It becomes harder to explain away, and the human mind tends to look for a deeper meaning. And what is your conclusion? "My mother is trying to tell me something!" But where are the facts to support this conclusion? There aren't any, are there?

We have all had these types of experiences. But what about the ones that are life changing? "I was going to buy that house, but I couldn't get the financing done… then a train ran right through it! I must have a guardian angel!" Or how about, "I heard someone yell out the name Jesus and I pulled in on my leash, and a car slid right up behind me just missing my dog…God was really looking out for us that day!" But is any of it proof of divine intervention? Does any of it mean that God is actively involved? Where does coincidence end and intent begin? How can we know?

I remember one instance where a couple of my friends and I were playing pool and we were discussing the music group "805," which was playing in town that night. Just then, the last three billiard balls on the table, the "8," the "5," and the cue ball, after being struck, lined up in the center of the table and came to a stop, all touching, in order: 8, cue ball, 5. Doesn't it seem hard to believe? Doesn't it seem even harder to believe that it was at 8:05 that night that it happened? I read the Bible a little while back. I read all of it. It took me almost three years. I finished on 11/11/11. Doesn't it seem hard to believe? Doesn't it seem even more fantastic that without any intent, I finished at exactly 11:00 a.m.? At what point does the fantastic mean something more? Does it mean that this "something more" is actively involved in our world, or does it mean that with all the variables available to us, coincidence will happen all the time?

Not long ago, I was sitting at a remote intersection in the winter at a stoplight. I was distracted with paperwork as the light changed green. I should have gone forward. Just then, a speeding minivan raced through the intersection, running the red light, on the way to the valley hospital doing over ninety miles an hour. I have no doubt in my mind that if I had proceeded forward, I would have been killed. So what stopped me that morning from doing what I have done on countless occasions before?

I am a rational man. I know that coincidences happen all the time. I know that logic says they mean nothing. I also know that there are a lot of very passionate people out there who are very quick to believe that they have meaning, that there are "guardian angels," loved ones who have passed on looking out for us, or God's loving hand. I refuse to align myself with those irrational individuals who pop off at every odd thing.

But, after having said that, I also find it impossible to explain away the oddities that I have seen as being just mere coincidences. There comes a time, when the nature or the magnitude of a strange occurrence defies logic to such an extreme that it has to be something more.

The part I didn't tell you about the day I finished the Bible? I was looking for meaning. But I was looking for that meaning in the Christmas song on the radio thinking that a major coincidence was imminent. As it turns out, it wasn't the radio at all, but the time. I felt like I was tricked, that there was intent. Logic, which very rarely lets me down, must be damned in this case. My feeling is now fact for me. And some of you will say, "Why? Just because of how reading the Bible ended for you?" And my answer is, "No, not how it ended...but what began when I finished reading the Bible!"

JUSTICE

THE CLOCK CONTINUES to move forward. Time is the measure of a person's life. And now as I get older, it has become apparent that there are some aspects of living that I just can't seem to get my arms around. Some of the things that frustrate me are stupidity, cruelty, and waste—waste of all sorts. But of all the things that seem to be beyond my grasp, one aspect of life, one philosophy, seems more cloudy and difficult to understand than any other. It is justice.

The idea of justice was not always looked at as it is now. It once had a much different meaning. The ancient Greeks defined *justice* as all parts of society doing their jobs. And when everyone is working and everything is in balance, society has justice. Think about it for a second—the policeman, the baker, the sanitation worker, the farmer, the soldier, all doing their job. Everything is balanced, hence justice.

Today in America, we look at justice in a different way. Justice today is bad people getting punished and good people succeeding. It is almost as if we are not happy unless the outcome follows the script of a John Wayne movie. And there is a part of me that feels "unbalanced" if justice is not served. It seems funny that the outcome of the two interpretations actually does mean the same thing.

But why does injustice make me upset? Imagine that while taking a test, if someone cheats and gets a passing grade when I had to study hard just to pass... well that's when I get angry. My sense of justice seems to be violated. I yearn for things to get straightened out. Then, when I realize it is out of my control, I try to convince myself that "God" or "nature" or the "flow of life" or "karma" will dispense the needed correction. And if that doesn't happen, I say to myself, "Give it time," because the bad guy eventually loses. But does he? What if he doesn't? That is when I do my Job impersonation (famous jilted Old Testament figure) by arguing with God.

But why do I do this? Why is it so important to me? Is it going to improve my week, or give me lower cholesterol? Obviously it is not going to directly affect me either way. Is it that I have an inner sense of how things should unfold? And when things don't follow my script, it gnaws at me. Luckily I am not the sort who feels a need to go out and fix these things myself, or I would probably end up as some masked vigilante stalking the streets at night.

But is there really justice? "Vengeance is mine, I will repay, saith the Lord" (Romans 12:19)…this sounds good. I want the speeder who cut me off to get a ticket. I want the bank robber to go to jail. I want the tax evader to get caught and the anonymous donator to come into money. I want the uncooperative customer who made me wait for ten minutes because he had to buy lottery tickets, cigarettes, and then paid with cash he couldn't find—in the express lane at the supermarket—I want that guy to get sprayed with water by a speeding car in the parking lot. But most of these things don't happen while I'm watching.

This is where someone who is spiritual needs to have faith in the order of things; to know that karma exists and is as unstoppable as water running down a hill. I would need to have confidence enough to say "They will get theirs one day" and really believe it. Does this mean that I lack faith in the order of things and how justice is dispensed? Yes, I think that is my problem. I lack faith.

I'm not sure what the cure for this is. Maybe it is because I'm not sure why I'm here. What is the point of my existence? How can I have faith that justice will happen when I don't know for sure? But then, why would we be programmed with such a high sense of justice if it wasn't important to someone or to the force that put us here?

Wouldn't it be ironic if I wasted much of my earthly existence worried about justice, only to find out from God after I was dead that the reason I was here had nothing to do with that at all? "Oh, so life was really about 'athletic competition,' and I chased around an imaginary guideline based on justice?" All the angels would laugh at me and God would give me some silly nickname. "Hey, Gabriel the Archangel, take a look at this idiot who wasted his party on earth! Let's nick-name this one Rube!"

Justice has gnawed at man for ages. Some of them were very good men and women, so I am in good company. And even back in ancient history, Job had the same problem thousands of years ago. Good thing for him, God took the time to straighten things out before he died. I don't think that will happen for me, however. (I lack faith, remember?) But there is one idea that helps me to cope with this imbalance. "Try not to worry about things you can't control." Unfortunately, this applies to most everything. Really life is an exercise for me to accept injustice more than anything else.

Maybe that is why John Wayne movies appeal to me? And not just me but to all those people who helped make them. They satisfy my sense of justice even when it is outside of my span of control. I don't know how this thing called life ends, and I don't know what comes next. But I must say I hope justice is as important to God as it is to me, or I'm going to look pretty silly on judgment day.

Nosce te Ipsum

A YOUNG MINISTER SAT in the park and quietly tried to understand why he felt the way he did. He did everything he could to help a troubled family. The family that he aided was grateful and he had made a difference. They had overcome their problems and now had moved away. "So why do I feel hollow?" he asked himself. He turned a small stick over and over in his hand as he sat on the park bench. Periodically he would break a piece off and throw it out onto the path in front of him.

He looked at the trees in the park as the wind blew. They would sway to the right while the leaves rustled. They would bend slightly from the trunk on up and then return to their former shape. He thought that deep down, that's what he had done during this whole ordeal. *Is that why I feel empty?* he wondered. Then he concluded that it wasn't that—it was something else. He was stumped. Self-inspection was a critical part for him to be good at his job, and so there was nothing left to do except to go see his father.

His father had retired a few years ago after a long career as a minister. He had so much experience with these things; surely he would be able to help him understand this emotion. The young minister dropped what remained of the small stick, stood up, took a deep breath, and began his trip across town to see his father.

He knew his father would be helpful, but he wished he could do this on his own. He had his own church now and he disliked conceding that he needed guidance. But under the circumstances, he felt that he had no other choice. "It's just my foolish pride," he said to himself as he got in his car.

Thirty minutes later, he stood at the front door of the apartment building. He hadn't had to get help from his father for almost two months. He would see him twice a week, but his visits wouldn't normally be work related. He had to prepare himself. He knew his father would question his unscheduled visit. He took a deep breath and then rang the bell.

A couple of minutes later, he was sitting in the living room with a cup of tea and staring out the window. His father, a little old man of seventy-two years, crossed the living room and sat in the chair next to his son. "You don't normally visit on Mondays," he said.

The young minister smiled lightly. The realization that they knew each other so well was comforting.

He answered, "I know...this is something else. I need advice." The old man took a sip of his tea. "Of course, my boy. What's wrong?" The young minister set the teacup down on the stand beside the chair, carefully making sure he did not spill it. He meticulously made sure it sat in the middle of the coaster. Then he began.

"You know the Reed family I was telling you about?"

"The family that just moved away?" answered his father.

"That's right. I feel very uneasy about my performance for some reason...and I don't know why."

The old Minister took another sip of his tea and rested it on his lap. "You'll have to tell me the details... if you want me to help." The young man really didn't want to. He didn't want to look bad in the eyes of his father, but now he didn't have any other choice.

He nodded. "The family had gotten into financial trouble. They had debt collectors threatening to evict them and to repossess their car. Michael Reed was too proud to ask for help, but his wife came to mass every week. She was very friendly and I liked her. She asked me if there was anything I could do. I gave her the money that I had saved for emergencies such as this." The young minister dropped his head. "I feel like I let my wife down. I feel like I let the whole church down. They took the money, fixed their problems, and moved away."

The old man needed more information. "Why do you feel that way?" he asked. The young man lifted his head. "I suspected that they were playing me. I was influenced by her beauty...I never should have given them that much money. They weren't from here, and it is surprising that they didn't stay."

The answer was clear to the old minister now. "First, my boy, you are not responsible for their actions…only your own. You helped a family in need. There is nothing wrong there. Second, you are a human being and you are not perfect. Every one of us has a line; this line is set and it says, 'This far is okay, but no farther.' When you cross the line, for whatever reason, it will make you uncomfortable. It is all about knowing who you are. We all draw those lines at different places. Some people are more in control than others. We reflect on events and we say, 'I shouldn't have done that,' and then we move the line. It is how we learn and improve ourselves. You found you have a weakness for a pretty woman? Welcome to the club." With that, the young minister smiled.

"So what have you learned?" asked the father. "Next time, give the money with a little more care and a little more thought. That is all there is to it."

The young man nodded. "So you are saying that I just need to know myself better? I should be aware of my weaknesses and improve on them?"

The old minister smiled. "That's right, my boy. Everyone has weaknesses. Admit to yourself that you have them and then improve on them. One day you may overcome them."

The young minister nodded and felt much better. "Dad…how did you get so wise?"

The old man sipped his tea and smiled. "I made a lot of mistakes."

Once upon a Memory

TIME IS A fascinating concept. It permits us to keep things in perspective. It not only allows us to understand our existence, but it also helps us to judge the significance of a contribution by how well it holds up to the test of time. Some things are remembered for centuries, while other things are only retained for a brief instance.

When we judge things that have happened in regard to time, it is safe to surmise that the most important things are remembered the longest, and the least significant things are quickly forgotten. I believe this tends to be true to an individual as well as to the entire history of mankind. The big difference between the two is that an individual may have a different way of judging personal memory than the way all of mankind may judge things. To put it in simpler terms, the things important to me are remembered with different significance than the things experienced by everyone else. Most of us know the name George Washington, but who remembers Danny Lambert? (He was a childhood friend of mine).

Things distort over time. Memories become less reliable. But we all have events that we remember that help to define who we are. They are the building blocks to the people we become. The point of this story is to retell a memory of mine from thirty-three years ago, partly because it was fun to experience and partly because it was an early indication of who I would become.

So now, the clock is rolling backward and we are approaching our destination. Here comes the signpost up ahead. It says, "Cypress Street," with an old brick school sitting just around a curve. The name is above the door in big letters and it says "Rome Catholic High School." The time is late May in the year 1979. The story begins with nineteen boys and a gym coach assembling just outside of the locker room for one of the last gym classes for this group of "seniors." It is an ugly group of awkward young men dressed in some of the most hideous athletic clothing ever designed. The only one who looks somewhat normal is the gym coach, Mike Davis.

Coach Davis was a successful running back for Idaho State during his college days and went on to coach football at Rome Catholic High. Later he would coach at Hamilton College before returning to Rome to coach football at RFA. Mike Davis loved football—old school, blood-and-guts football where you were expected to give everything you had, lose a leg, and still somehow try to make the tackle. Mike Davis did not tolerate excuses or laziness. And if there is one thing that can be said about this man "Mugsy"—named because of his large mustache—he *hated* to lose at anything. He would battle you at ping pong like it was the Olympics and you were on the Chinese national team. One other thing—he looked like he was still playing football. He worked out more than the players on his football team, I think.

Now I never played football in high school; that's organized football. My friends and I would play all the time during the fall and winter in parking lots and open fields. That was the extent of my football career. The reason why is because baseball was my life's love; that is what I played at every organized level available to me and that is what I focused on. I did not want to commit to a game where I could get hurt and miss out on baseball. So Mike Davis and the football team, which was pretty successful for a small school, was only something I watched.

So on this particular day, which I think was the next to last gym class I ever had, Mike Davis greets the senior boys and says, "I have a treat for you today! For gym class, we are going to break up into two teams and go outside and play football on the football field. Tackle football!" Of course, the young men are excited. We were never allowed to do this for fear of someone getting hurt. But old Mugsy wants to share his life's love with these boys before they move on in life.

The first thing to do is to select two captains to pick the teams. Naturally, Coach Davis gives the first honor to Jack Roberts—quarterback of the football team and best athlete in the class. The second captain picked was me, captain and shortstop of the baseball team. Now Jack is taller, stronger, faster, and could throw harder than I could, but I had a more accurate arm. Coach Davis gives Jack the first pick, and of course he picks Timmy Schmandt, the running back on the football team. Now I get the next two picks. I picked my best friend Phillip Schiederich who wasn't the best athlete around, but he had skills. He was only on "special teams" with football, but he was someone whom I played football with all the time on the weekends.

Now Mugsy sees that the teams are going to be unbalanced, so he jumps forward and says "By the way, I'm playing!"

I reiterated. "You're playing, Coach?"

He said, "Yup, I'm playing!" and rather emphatically, I might add.

I said, "Okay…I'll take Bauer!" The whole gym burst out in laughter and Coach Davis dropped his head and said "Shesssss!" Mike Bauer was a basketball dropout, but he was my friend and together we managed to survive in high school. Of course, Jack took Mugsy next.

The team selection went back and forth, and to describe it in simple terms, the football team players with Mike Davis were on one side and me and my friends were on the other. So the nineteen boys and the gym coach trot outside and the kickoff starts the game. The very first play, I get elbowed in the head, and I realize, *Hey, these guys think it's a real high school football game... without the pads.*

For the next forty-five minutes, the two teams square off and inflict pain upon each other. I remember one goal line stance when John Fitzgerald tried to run in a short touchdown. I grabbed him with my left arm but I couldn't hold him. He started to spin toward the goal line. Just then, little Paul Issom slammed into him, dropping him on the one-yard line.

I remember the football team talking smack. They were going to mop the field with us. I remember Terry Waite yelling for the ball on one play because I cut underneath him while covering him in a pass pattern. To this day, I think it was the right choice. The teams went back and forth, and surprisingly the score was tied—two touchdowns apiece—when Coach Davis announced "Next score wins!"

Mugsy's team drove down to the five-yard line and they were threatening to win the game. Coach Davis called the play. Jack Roberts took the snap and lateralled the ball to Coach Davis. He rolled left parallel to the goal line. Two receivers from the other team ran along with him just inside the end zone. I was covering the front receiver with another trailing me by about two yards.

Coach Davis threw the ball trying to connect to the trailing receiver. I reached back with my left hand and speared the tip of the football with my fingers and pulled it in. Then I turned up field and went the whole one hundred yards for the winning touchdown. When I had gone eighty yards, I knew no one was following me, so I trotted the last twenty. Naturally, I spiked the ball with complete disdain for the filthy pigskin and then went into my version of a disco dance for the benefit of both teams. It was a moment of glory in the eyes of a young man. I knew it really meant very little, but boy was it satisfying.

Now the tired and sweaty young men make their way back into the gym. It leaves Coach Davis alone on the field with the football. We were all laughing in the locker room because we could hear him through the walls. He spent the next ten minutes screaming outside, throwing the ball into the brick building. He really hated to lose.

Of course very few would remember that game; some of those boys aren't even alive anymore. But I learned something of myself that day. First, I realized that I was a good judge of character. Second, I learned that when people are properly motivated, they can accomplish great things. And third, I knew that dancing was always going to be a challenge for me.

And one more thing..."In your face, Mugsy!"

Only Lions Roar

COPPER LOOKED AT the root in his den. It had a nice curve to it as it came out of the wall. It created the perfect angle for his back. He turned in a circle and then curled into his spot. He wanted to sleep but he knew it wasn't going to be that simple tonight. He took a deep breath and let it out slowly. He closed his eyes and tried to clear his mind. He could hear footsteps in the adjoining room. He knew the argument was only moments away. He stayed motionless anyway.

Sandy sniffed and knew exactly where he was. She stood in the doorway and paused before she spoke. She was not surprised, just disappointed. She did not understand. She started to speak but then hesitated. She wanted to say the right thing, but she wasn't sure what the right thing was, so she decided to keep it simple.

"Copper, what are you doing?" she asked even though she already knew the answer.

He decided to avoid the topic. "Trying to sleep," he said. His eyes remained closed.

"But why? Our family needs your voice tonight?" Copper immediately knew that wasn't true. She just likes the attention, the popularity, and the controversy. The outcome doesn't really matter to her.

"Sandy, you know as well as I do that nothing will be resolved tonight. Nothing ever is."

She knew that her last approach was a dead end, so she decided to try a different one. "Don't you want our children to be proud of you? Don't you think you need to be an example for them? What will their friends say?" Copper did not try to answer. He realized that he hadn't considered that before.

Sandy is trying really hard tonight, he thought.

Copper was not in the mood to debate this topic again. He had lived with Sandy for years. He had hoped that one day she would accept him for who he was and that she would stop trying to make him into someone else. He rolled over onto his other side. She knew it was his way of saying "Let it go."

Sandy could smell the blood on his shoulder. Copper had a spider bite that was bothering him. "Do you want me to clean that for you?" she asked.

"No...I just want to sleep," he replied.

Sandy sighed. "Well, if you're not going to come, I'll just have to go to the meeting alone..." The comment did not draw a response. Sandy was disappointed with Copper again. And even though she was bothered by his lack of interest, there was never any doubt about how much she cared about him. She quietly crossed the room and nuzzled her face up to his. Then she left him there alone in the dark curled up in his favorite spot.

Sandy got to the meeting and found the chamber very crowded. She recognized most of the families in attendance as she was related to a number of them. Each family had a spokesperson, and it didn't take long before the meeting became loud. She did not speak during the entire event but she did show her approval by spinning. A couple of times, when a point was well made, she stood as high as she could to show her support. The last half of the meeting got ugly. A couple of fights broke out, and most of those involved were yelling very loudly. Sandy decided it was time to leave.

By the time she got home, it was well past dark. She came into the den where Copper was lying and sniffed his shoulder. "This is healing fine," she said, loud enough to wake him. His eyes opened but he said nothing. She wanted him to ask about the meeting, so she gave him a minute. He knew what she wanted and he remained silent.

"The meeting went well. Until the end, that is. A couple of fights broke out. My sister's husband made some good points...You know, Copper, our family has stopped asking where you are. I think they'd be surprised if you did go to a meeting."

Without moving his head, he said, "Was anything resolved?"

Sandy was ready for the question. "Nothing gets fixed over night," she stated. Copper made it a point to say nothing more.

Sandy began to leave the room and then decided to ask one more question. She turned from the entrance. "Why don't you like the meetings?"

Copper was momentarily stunned. It was such a simple question, but the answer was anything but simple. It would be a "window to the soul" moment for Copper. He decided to be open and honest. Sandy deserved that.

"It's not that I don't like the idea of making things better. I want things to be better, just like everyone else. But I like me the way I am. Crowds make listeners believe things they don't really believe in. The excitement and the speeches get people all riled up. It gives an excuse to do things and be someone you're not. That's how riots form. That's why large crowds get out of hand. I don't like losing myself, or letting a crowd turn me into someone that I'm not. People get so mad, then it leads to fights and hard feelings. And for what? Maybe I can change things by being an example of how we should act."

Sandy nodded. "You know, Copper, people listen to a loud voice; that's why lions roar. Why can't you be more like a lion? And not as quiet as a..." His head shot up and she stopped.

"I am who I am, Sandy." She was ashamed of her attack on him. Deep down, she respected him. A tear welled in her eye, and she left the room to go attend to the children.

Copper thought there had to be a way to change things, a way to move forward past the crowd and the arguments. He knew Sandy didn't agree with his perspective. He was tired of these discussions. There were far too many meetings and not enough action taken. Copper was lost in these thoughts.

Patiently, silently, and slowly, his son snuck into the room. He made his way along the north side of the chamber. He was almost upon him before Copper knew he was there. "Shadow? What's wrong?" asked Copper as his head popped up. His son rushed forward and he nudged his cheek. "I think you roar, Daddy." He curled up next to his father and began to nibble at the corn that was lying next to him. "When I grow up, I want to be just like you."

Copper suddenly realized he could make a difference, and he could do it his way, even if it only meant his children would grow up to be strong and brave. He briefly thought of bringing his son back to Sandy in the children's chamber, but then he changed his mind. He knew it was going to be a cold night. *When you grow up, I believe you will roar, Shadow!* he thought. *But right now, I just want you to stay my warm little mouse.*

Show Me

HAVE YOU EVER wondered why we accept the things that surround us? We are taught lessons, phrases, trivia, the language, math, history, morals, social norms, etiquette, speech, athletics, nature, and the list goes on and on. And very rarely do we go back and review what we use as our foundation for the information we base our lives on.

It is true that as we mature we outgrow some things like Santa Claus and the tooth fairy. We even learn "real" history after we leave high school. But for the most part, we do not question things we have set as our foundation. And then when they do come into question and we are forced to think about them, we seem confused and somewhat embarrassed that we hadn't considered it before. That we had become complacent and stale.

The idea of purchasing water is a good place to begin. When I was little, I would go out and play all day without going home. In the summer, we would play baseball and kickball and hide and seek from 9 a.m. until 9 p.m. And if we got thirsty, we would go to someone's garden hose and get a drink of water. And if we were lucky enough to have some money, we would go to the little store on the corner and get a spectacular bottle of soda. Soda you paid for, water you got from a garden hose.

When the idea of purchasing water from a bottle began, it seemed comical to me. Why would anyone want to pay for water when it comes out of your faucet? I have now accepted the idea that people pay for water. But…I will not pay for water. I've had to reconsider the perception of water and how to obtain it, and I never saw it coming. So many aspects of our lives are being turned upside down, that a lot of it is disappearing right before our eyes. Phone booths/pay phones, encyclopedias, phone books, maps, newspapers, cursive writing, the mail, repair shops, corner stores, and the home phone are being replaced by mini marts, cell phones, computers, and industrial improvements right now as you read this. I am convinced that these changes will continue to evolve, and it will make my childhood look even more primitive than it does right now.

But the point of this story is not the changes in the world, but rather one simple idea that I've recently reassessed and realized that I had it wrong. My original interpretation of this idea was accepted, digested and minimized and then stored away. I recently have had to consider a relationship that was bothering me, and it forced me to pull it out, dust it off, and look at it again. And to my surprise, I realized I had made a mistake.

It is the simple idea of "show me." The idea was originally aligned in my brain as the state motto of Missouri. I originally valued its meaning to be associated with cynics and skeptics, that it was just a way to say "people can't be trusted to tell things accurately" and that the vast majority of storytellers embellish and distort the reality of events for their own self-interests. And it was at this point that the idea was accepted as accurate and stored away. But with the changing conditions of my life I've had to reexamine the idea. And that is when I came to the conclusion that I missed the larger meaning.

The concept of "show me" could mean what I previously described, but it could very well mean that the original intention of this concept wasn't meant for it to be the motto of cynics and skeptics. It is quite possible that the idea has a different meaning altogether.

I was trying to understand the lack of dedication people have to ideals that they contend to support. Many individuals, whom I have had dealings with, say that they believe in or have the intention to correct an injustice, but that is where their involvement ends. They explain and confirm the problem, they make a lot of noise about the issue, but then they do nothing.

It is at that point my mind suddenly blurted out, *Don't tell me you support this idea…show me you support it!* I quickly realized that I had redefined the concept of "show me." It wasn't that I doubted the truth of an event, but that I was putting a greater emphasis on action instead of on intention.

There are a number of other sayings that convey this thought using different words such as "Put up or shut up," "Put your money where your mouth is," "Money talks and bullshit walks," "There is a big difference between knowing the path and walking the path," and "The smallest good deed is worth more than the grandest good intention." They all call into play the importance of "doing." So, in other words, "Don't tell me what you think, show me what you think." And what a completely different implication that this small two-word phrase brings with it to the counter.

It now draws out the chapter of James in the Bible. Jesus's half brother explains that it isn't what you think or read or say that defines who you are, but it is what you do that defines you." It now puts the emphasis on action rather than words. It now means that I will judge you by your deeds rather than by your intentions.

In all truthfulness, I never really liked the slogan "show me" as I previously interpreted it. It had large negative connotations and seemed to only apply to the shallow relationships between scammers and those who were scammed. It seemed to fit at carnivals and auctions. It was a phrase directed to snake-oil salesmen and fortune-tellers. The person who blurted it out was alone in his or her island and looked at the rest of the word through eyes of mistrust and theft.

This new definition now directs it toward action instead of to intent. It forces someone to prove their words. It tells those who lack motivation to "get up and out of bed in the morning and start living." It now points out that far too many people watch things happen as they drift away on the couch, watching "reality shows" do their living for them. It tells young people to get off the computer, to get out from behind the video game, to put down the cell phone and go out and *do* something to make a difference.

Our world is in danger of becoming one that is laced in memory and storytelling. It is becoming an arena where people long to be entertained by everything from sports, to movies, to politics and current events; that we are now becoming lost in a phony lazy life of contented inaction. It reminds me of an insidious ancient political tactic known as "Bread and Circus," where the intention was to keep a poor people entertained and quiet. We need to take a different look at how we function and what we do with our lives. We need to "get in the game" and live.

I'm trying politely to tell you to get up, get out of that chair, and go make a difference. Play baseball with your grandkids. Plant a garden down at the hospital. Help your church at the chicken barbeque. And if you get thirsty while you are doing it, go get a drink from a garden hose. Go out there and make a difference with your life. And don't just say you're going to do it… show me!

The Debate

THE UNIVERSE IS larger than comprehension, and yet it is God's backyard. God sees everything. And today his attention is captured by a complex situation on earth. A man was confronted with a question of personal honor. He had a choice between personal wealth and being looked at as a disloyal cheat. His only penalty would be to lose the respect of his former company. He took the money. God began to wonder why people have such little regard for their own souls.

God created the race of man in his own image, but as his children, he had wanted them to develop, to evolve and to grow to a higher standard. He had hoped man would strive to become more like him. Instead they spend way too much time worshipping wealth. There had to be a way to correct this flaw, but in order to correct it, God needed to understand the details behind it.

Michael the archangel stood before his Lord and immediately knelt. "You wish something of me, my Lord?" he asked.

"Michael, I need to understand what motivates the race of men."

Michael nodded. "Yes, Lord….they are complex."

God said, "Hmmpf, I need an arena"—he spun a small blue flower in his right hand—"one where this can be explained."

Michael looked up. "A debate, Lord? You could invite two opposing points of view and have them defend their values…or lack of values."

God liked the idea. Michael continued, "But the two opposing sides must not be aware that it is a viewed debate, or it will alter the validity of the discussion." God looked down at Michael and smiled. "Sorry, Lord. I knew you already knew that. But who would be qualified to argue for either side?" God looked down on earth and knew what he was looking for. It only took him a brief moment to find the pair that he needed. He then invited five more of his angels to add to the debate.

Michael was always fascinated by God's wisdom. He knew God had a special love for humanity. Michael had been tracking their progress for thousands of years. He had seen the race of man develop through many different ages. Some things he came to anticipate and understand; other things he never understood. One of the things he could never get used to was the styles they choose for clothing. Michael knew that this show would be an entertaining and he looked forward to the part he would play.

The door to the meeting room opened, and a man dressed in a gray suit turned the lights on. He was a medium-sized man, close to retirement age, with white hair and glasses. He wore a blue tie, and his suit was old and frayed in a couple of spots. He held a small briefcase in one hand as he stood by the window and waited. Not long after, another man entered the room and closed the door. He was a younger man and wore a dark suit with a red tie. He had black hair, a somewhat muscular frame, and walked with confidence. He also carried a small briefcase. "Hey Sidney, what time is Benson supposed to be here?"

The older man turned to the younger one and answered, "Hello, Alex. The chairman said he'd be here a little after 10 a.m. That means we have about ten minutes to wait." Alex nodded, looked at his expensive Swiss watch, and then pulled out a chair and slid into it.

"I'm gonna propose site 'A.' I think it might be a public image gamble, but the profit margin will be through the roof."

Sidney seemed stunned. "Alex…you can't be serious? We'd have to displace forty families…not to mention what we could potentially do to the drinking water in the neighborhood." Alex waved his hand at Sidney to minimize his response. "It's worth the bad press, Sidney. I've thought it through and it's what I'm proposing. You go ahead and tell them to pick site 'D'...it would help my career."

Sidney knew this was all about Alex getting that promotion. He shook his head in disbelief. "Alex...it's not about money here; it's about doing the right thing," he responded.

The younger man seemed insulted. "Who's to say what the right thing is, Sidney? Who anointed you as neighborhood guardian? I'm looking at the big picture for the company. How many corporate families will it help?"

Sidney replied, "I'm looking out for the company too! And the company you see is not the company I want to be associated with."

Alex shook his head. "You should have retired with the last buyout, Sidney."

Right then the door opened, and the chairman of the board came in. Alex jumped out of the chair and said, "Good morning, Mr. Benson!" He was followed into the room by six other corporate men and women. They went straight into the adjoining meeting room and took their seats. It was a large room, and the meeting table was very long and very expensive. Sidney sat on one side of the far end of the table and Alex sat across from him. They both set their briefcases in front of them and opened them up. Mr. Benson sat at the end of the table with his six associates sitting close to him, three on each side. He looked around the table to make sure everyone was situated. Once he was satisfied, he said, "Okay, let's get started. How is everyone doing?" His six associates smiled, but Alex and Sidney looked very stiff. "You two fellows are both supposed to have a site proposal recommendation for our new production facility, correct?"

Alex and Sidney both nodded. They looked very different but they both shared the same nervous look. The other members around the table stared at them in anticipation. Mr. Benson pulled in his seat closer to the table, leaned forward, and asked, "So...who wants to go first?" In that instant, the room was especially quiet. One could almost hear the pressure upon the two men who were preparing to make their presentations.

Alex looked at Sidney, and Sidney stared back at Alex. Both men swallow hard and together they both turned in unison looking toward the head of the table at Mr. Benson. He sat there with a smile on his face and was completely motionless, except for the small blue flower that he spun in his right hand.

The Doorman

THE SKY SUDDENLY lit up from a bolt of lightning, and it was quickly followed by a crash of thunder that filled the night air. The heavy rain pounded the city streets forcing those unlucky enough to be outside to run from cab to awning. The rainwater ran down the streets in small streams and twisted and gurgled down partially clogged drains all over the city.

Ernie stood a distance from the doorway of the Barton Building just outside the protection of the walkway awning under a "golfer's" umbrella waiting for the next person who needed him. Ernie was a large man in height and in weight. His hair was white now as Father Time began to bear down on him, but still he was an imposing figure even for his age.

You would think that a man such as this would be known for his unusual size, but that was not the case with "old Ernie." He was known for having the kind of smile that would change your day. He had a way of making the most miserable and unhappy people feel better just because he was there.

He had been the doorman at this building longer than what most people could remember. He knew everyone who resided within, and he knew an even larger number of people who used to reside within. Ernie was exceptionally good with names. He was even better with faces, and he had the kind of effect on people that made them want to remember him.

Just then a cab pulled up to the curb and it came to a splashing stop in the middle of a large puddle. Ernie recognized Mr. Thompson right away. He was a fat, middle-aged businessman who worked late hours. It wasn't unusual for him to come home long past dark and tonight he had the misfortune of a long drive in a rainstorm. Ernie tried to pace his arrival to the door of the cab with Mr. Thompson's normal pace of egress. He knew there would be an argument over the cab fair because that was his nature, so Ernie gave Mr. Thompson an extra minute before going to the cab door. He didn't want the fat businessman to think "Old Ernie" was waiting for him. Such was his nature.

Ernie was attentive to his job to a higher level than most people could even appreciate. Every day he went to work prepared. He showed great attention to every detail. He had five suits and they were always clean. He wore shined shoes and white socks every day he worked. But the thing that made Ernie special was the other things.

Ernie always brought six dog biscuits, four lollipops, a pack a cigarettes, a lighter, two clean handkerchiefs and a towel—and he did this five days a week. I will not waste your time explaining this pattern, but believe me when I tell you that every one of these things had a purpose. Their purpose wasn't based on a work requirement. It was based on people—friends of his, little kids he cared about, little dogs who could use some love, and a handful of lonely souls he took care of.

Ernie had dreams of being a football player when he was young. He was big and fast in high school, but one bad hit to his left knee ended that dream. He went straight from high school to the Barton Building. He was liked so much by the owner that he had been in the same position for forty-six years. Not a day went by that Ernie didn't think about what he should have done with his life. We all have dreams, and Ernie had big dreams. *Maybe big men have bigger dreams?* thought Ernie as he held the umbrella for Mr. Thompson.

Ernie grabbed the hand of the fat businessman and helped him to cross the large mud puddle that the taxi had navigated so poorly. They walked through the pouring rain to the door of the Barton Building. Ernie opened the door with the large smile that was his trademark. Mr. Thompson had been in a miserable mood but suddenly, as he tried to absorb the onslaught of the doorman's personality, he melted into a pool of exhausted relief. He knew he was home and safe. "Thanks, Ernie! What would we do without you?" said Mr. Thompson with a silly grin.

"You are most welcome, sir!" he replied as he tipped his hat. It was what he always replied.

The rain stopped around midnight and it was time for Ernie to go home. He walked down the street the short distance to his apartment building. He greeted two girls who were hard at work, and he concluded another successful day at the Barton Building.

The next day, Ernie started his shift at 4 p.m. and the weather was much better than the day before. Ernie actually preferred rainy days because he felt more needed, but dry evenings were good too. People loved to stop and talk to "Old Ernie." Ernie had no sooner assumed his post and straightened his hat when Mrs. James turned from the lobby to the door with her little dog Nelson. It was a strange name for a dog, but Ernie never mentioned it to Mrs. James. He patted the little Yorkie on the head, slipped him a dog biscuit, and then opened the door with his signature smile. Mrs. James said, "Thank you, Ernie. You are the best," and Ernie replied, "You are most welcome, ma'am," as he tipped his hat.

Sometimes life unfolds slowly; other times it comes crashing in like a stone trough a factory window. Ernie had just stepped outside when he noticed a woman chasing her baby carriage. The large old doorman instinctively broke into the street. His football instincts came back to him as he lowered his shoulder and knocked two men out of the way. Ernie threw himself in front of the carriage deflecting it just enough to miss the oncoming bus and pushing it softly and miraculously to a stop on the curb.

If only Ernie had been so lucky. The bus made full contact with his chest and had crushed his ribcage. "Old Ernie" lay there in the street with blood on his mouth and on his suit. It was the first time in forty-six years that Ernie was dirty while at work. The light in his eyes went out as he looked at the baby carriage that had come to a rest in front of him. He could hear the baby crying, and he knew he had made a difference. Ernie died with that big smile on his face.

The next day, it was business as usual at the Barton Building as the world went on with life. A new doorman stood at the doorway and to a stranger, it seemed normal. But everyone who lived there knew the personality of the neighborhood had changed. Ernie had thought he missed out on his calling, but the truth of the matter is Ernie made a difference every day of his life. Not because of wealth, or power, or success, but because he was a role model to so many on how to be a good man. Later that day, the resident of that stray baby carriage, William Roby, who was a rather large baby boy with an abnormally large smile, was renamed Ernest William Roby.

THE FOOL

A LONG TIME AGO, in a remote kingdom on the edge of a great forest, lived a very lonely prince. The prince was well respected and excelled in just about every skill necessary to be a future king. As a matter of fact, the only thing common about the prince was his name "Andrew" and the fact that he was lonely.

The king was getting old, and Andrew was his only son. Now that Andrew was getting close to ascending to the throne, the king worried that his land would not have a queen once he and his wife were gone. The king and queen constantly introduced him to the richest and prettiest young woman in the kingdom, but

Andrew could not find one whom he could see as his future queen.

He thought most of the girls were too young, too foolish, or too interested in the throne. He wanted a partner and someone whom he respected. He looked for someone who would be a good mother, a good queen, and a companion for him to battle the challenges of life with. None of the women he met ever seemed to measure up. His father joked that his mother had put "the bar too high."

So one day, the king called his advisors together to solve this problem. His throne room was large, and the eight people who were present heard their words echo off of the walls in the large chamber. The king began by presenting his concern, and his wife who sat by his side nodded in agreement while she held his hand.

His military advisor said, "Sire, we should have a big celebration to commemorate our victories and invite the most beautiful and accomplished eligible woman from the kingdom to meet the prince."

The king shook his head no. "We've already tried that, Cedric!"

His foreign advisor said, "Sire, why don't we invite the neighboring kingdoms for a peace conference and use the event to invite the royal princesses from across the land?"

The king nodded no again. "We've already tried that, too, Phineus!"

His finance minister was next. "Sire, what about having a bazaar? We could invite the wealthiest families and their daughters?"

The king was getting frustrated as he shook his head no again. "That's been done, too, Phillip!" he said.

His religious advisor stepped forward. "Sire, the feast of summer solstice is coming. Why not invite all the local churches to the castle? There are many daughters of the church out there who have many of the qualities that the prince is looking for."

The king shook his head no again. "We did that in the spring, William!"

His progress minister was last. "Sire, we should have a beauty pageant with a great prize! That would surely get the prince's attention."

The King shook his head no one more time. "That's not what the boy is looking for, Thomas!" The King stood as his anger and frustration began to boil over.

"I rely on the five of you to help me run this kingdom and not one of you has an idea on how to proceed?" Just then, his court jester sprung to his feet. He danced in a circle, and the seven of them all turned to look at him. The small bells on his feet jingled as he waddled and spun like a top about to fall over.

"Oh, Sire, the answer is simple. Only a fool can straighten this out." The seven of them laughed. The very idea that wisdom would come from the jester was comical.

"And what, pray tell, is the answer, Edgar?" inquired the king.

The jester stopped spinning and balanced himself on one foot while the other hung in the air in front of him. His arms were spread to his sides and his floppy hat hung almost over his eyes. "Send him on a quest to nowhere! He will find his love!"

The seven of them looked at the clown with their mouths open. No one said a word. Then, the king slowly sat back down on his throne. "William, I want you to spread word that the royal crest has been stolen." They all looked at the crest which was hanging on the wall behind the throne.

"Cedric, I want ten of your best soldiers to accompany my son on his quest. Phillip, I want you to put together supplies and staff for twenty-five people for a one-month journey. Thomas, I need fourteen of your best support staff for this trip. Phineus, I want you to hide the family crest in the dungeon."

The king then turned to his wife. "My queen, fetch our son." The room stood motionless. The king said firmly "You have your assignments…go!" The six people quickly rose and scattered to follow the king's instructions. Soon just the king and his jester were left in the throne room. Edgar continued to balance himself on one foot.

"That was unexpected. I wouldn't have thought a fool would have given me the best advice," chided the king.

Edgar smiled. "That is why you are a great king… not many people would recognize wisdom from a fool."

Two weeks later, the prince returned from his quest. He did not find the family crest, but he did find his bride to be. It turns out she was one of the king's loyal subjects and the daughter of one of the soldiers that went on the quest. She was smart, strong, good-natured, and she liked the prince for who he was, not for what he offered.

The king sat in his garden with his wife and watched the sun set. Edgar stood on a ledge of flowers and tried not to fall. The king shook his head at his antics. "I think I deserve a promotion!" said Edgar as he tumbled into the flowers. The king shook his head. "No, Edgar. You are perfect right where you are—by my side."

THE FORTUNE-TELLER

A MIDDLE-AGED MAN STANDS in front of a gray tent and impatiently waits for a much younger woman. She reaches out for his hand and nearly stumbles as her high heels dig into the soft earth. Apparently she had not planned on traversing this sort of terrain on this date. He grabs a hold of the tent flap and he impolitely enters before his female companion. He walks toward a small round table in the center of the room as the female manages to quickly emerge back at his side. Four unoccupied chairs surround the table. It is covered with a large green tablecloth that droops down and almost reaches the floor. The only thing on this table is a crystal ball which stays in place, thanks to a small black stand. It sits there propped up alone and majestically implying that something mysterious is waiting.

The couple walks slowly toward the table as they scan the room for the fortune-teller. The girl is laughing and clinging to the man like a high school girl. The man bursts out in a loud deep voice, "What a stinking dump! Hello? Is anybody here?" He is obviously in a hurry. He wears a suit and struts as if he has power in his life.

A little old man wearing a white outfit waddles toward them from the back of the tent. Omar, the gypsy, appears to be of Middle Eastern descent. A slight smile crosses his face as the prospect of learning something more about life crosses his mind. He stops at a small desk and swings a red-and-black cape around his back, and he slowly and methodically fixes his hair in preparation for a turban.

"Come on, Gramps! We haven't got all day!" The man yells as the little old fortune-teller fixes his costume. The old man, who seems impervious to the rudeness of his customers, returns a smile to them. His response says "This isn't my first rodeo." The young woman becomes even more childlike as she wraps herself around the man's waist. Apparently his status is exciting to her. Her status to him, on the other hand, seems more like a nuisance.

The old fortune-teller motions for them to sit, then he says, "Oh, Omar, where is your mind this day?" as he snaps his fingers. He slowly steps back to his desk to put his medallion on around his neck. The man at the table is now agitated, and he blurts out, "Jesus Christ, will you look at this guy? We only have two hours together, and this guy is going to kill it all before he even gets to the damn table!" The young girl laughs hard and puts her head on his shoulder while they impatiently sit there waiting.

The fortune-teller is about to sit, and he notices the man has a wedding ring on his hand but the young girl does not. He sits at the table and says, "Are you ready to begin?"

The man scoffs and says, "Yeah. How about you do me first?"

The fortune teller nods. He leans forward to the crystal ball. He waves his hands over the glass orb and says a few words in a language unfamiliar to his two guests. Then with his hands extended but now motionless, he closes his eyes. After a few moments, his eyes reopen and he says, "You will die a lonely man. Few will attend your funeral. And after your death, you will be forgotten quickly."

The man suddenly considers this horrible legacy and says, "You see that in the crystal ball? It looks the same to me as it did before..."

The old man smiles and says, "No....it is just a piece of glass."

The Last Clue

LEON HAD BEEN with the police force for twenty-eight years. He had moved up the ranks, starting as a beat cop. He was now one of the most respected homicide detectives in the city. He worked hard, put in long hours, and was known as the "Tiger of 42nd Street." He earned the nickname because he had the highest percentage of solved murder cases in the last twenty years, and the press loved the spectacle around his cases.

About two years ago, Leon solved a high-profile murder on 42nd Street when it looked like the media had the suspected culprit dead to rights. Leon stayed with the case until he proved another man was the perpetrator. The press compensated for their "rush to judgment" by anointing Leon as something special.

Leon never bought into the hype. He was thorough, studied his cases, and was willing to do the dirty details that others shied away from. That's the real reason why he was successful. His approach to the job yielded results and that gave him confidence. And even though he secretly liked the media attention, it was not what motivated him. His real motivation flowed from his parents teaching him about "right and wrong." He acknowledged that he had an overinflated sense of justice.

Leon had done this for a long time and now he was close to retiring. The precinct took that into consideration but they had assigned him a high-profile murder investigation anyway. It was over three months old now and the trail had gone stale. The police commissioner was getting heat from the mayor to solve it, so as a last resort he brought in Leon.

Leon had begun studying it right away. After two weeks of intense scrutiny from "The Tiger of 42nd Street," every avenue, every possible lead seemed to run into a dead end. A doctor was murdered at a big office party. There were some fifty-one people in attendance, and close to thirty of these were related to the deceased. So many possible motives and so many possible opportunities made this case extremely difficult to solve.

The doctor had been stabbed in the chest. There were no fingerprints and the knife itself led them nowhere. The doctor's last words were "If Solomon was wise, what does that make David?" Leon had hoped it would be the clue to cracking the case. The only problem was that of the fifty-one people at the party, not one of them was named Solomon or David. There weren't even any relatives in town named David, and this frustrated Leon.

There were security cameras mounted in a number of places in the building, but none contributed to unraveling the crime. The doctor was a famous plastic surgeon. The crime was committed in a side office. No one knew why he had gone in there and he wasn't discovered until he was nearly dead. The cameras showed the guests moving all through the building before, during, and after the stabbing, but nothing indicated anything significant.

Leon had looked over the personal history of each of the fifty-one possible suspects. It was a lot of work. He identified ten strong suspects and another ten with a possible motive, but none of that information got him closer to the answer. Leon pulled out every approach he knew of but nothing seemed to help. He wanted to throw his hands up and admit defeat, but his stubbornness would not allow that.

He had just finished reading file number fifty-one for the third time and once again he found nothing. He wanted to go down to the local bar and forget this case. He hoped there was one last clue. He remembered a movie he saw once. In that film, the final criminal was tripped up because of a cold. Leon suddenly felt that someone must have made a mistake in that party somewhere. There must be some kind of error that would give him away, and all he had to do was find it.

He decided to watch the security camera footage one more time.

He had already looked at all the tapes multiple times but never with the idea of looking for an instance where somebody betrayed themselves. He wasn't sure what he was looking for, but just maybe there was some detail he missed. Leon queued up the first camera and began to watch. He saw all kinds of people involved. There were men, women, old people and young kids. He saw arguments and laughing. There was a lot of alcohol and a lot of food. He saw nothing suspicious, and there was nothing that seemed out of place.

Then he thought of the movie scene again: There was a sneeze that couldn't be controlled—gesundheit—and that gave him away! Leon had the right frame of mind now; all he needed was something that didn't fit in. He switched tapes to the camera mounted outside the front door. He would watch people come in. He felt that was a good place to start.

Two men entered—*cousins I think*— then three co-workers. *Drunk already*, he thought. Then the victim's parents came in. *Father holds the door for his wife. Next, his brother and his wife rush in. He holds the door for his wife as she hurries through in an attempt to catch up to their parents.* It all seems pretty normal to Leon.

More people enter—caterers, coworkers, an aunt and uncle. *Barney and Betty, just like the Flintstones*, thinks Leon as he lets out a brief chuckle. He still has learned nothing after twenty minutes. Two cousins are next, *Shelly and Darlene*, remembers Leon. *Nothing there*, he thinks and then moves on. He watches for another minute when suddenly the little hairs on the back of his neck stand up. In a brief hesitation, he hits pause on the tape player, then he hits the rewind button. He goes back before the two cousins and then forward again.

Here comes Darlene. She opens the door. She holds it. She lets Shelly go in first. Leon thinks *Strange...it reminds me of Betty and Barney. Oh...but Darlene? You were more than polite, weren't you?* "I think you were!" yells Leon even though he is the only one in the room.

He quickly gets on the phone. He makes call after call. He frantically tries to verify a suspicion. He writes a date "3/22/10" on a pad of paper, and then he writes the word "surgery." He scribbles a name. He crosses it out. He writes another name. Leon slams down the phone and then leaps from his chair to go get a car. He runs out of the room; his face is red and his heart is pounding.

As Leon races down the stairs, he realizes that people can hide what they do and they can change what they look like, but you can't change who you are. The "Tiger of 4nd Street" will keep his title tonight, and by tomorrow his name will be on the headlines again.

For on the little piece of paper, the last two names give the answer. Scrawled in poor handwriting is the name "Darlene" with a line through it, and next to that is the name "David."

The Legacy of Ego

HAVE YOU EVER noticed that once a person gets past the midlife crisis stage of their life, the idea of what they have left behind when they are gone seems to become more and more important as the end draws closer? The concept of "legacy" affects most people. I will grant you that it means more to some more than others, but having said that, it appears to influence and dominate the motivations of even the most undisciplined and lethargic individuals right along with the most genuine and caring souls.

This concern in the later years of life has affected me too. It is now far more important what I leave behind as I get closer to the end. It has forced me to be more introspective. It forces a conflict within me where I now have to incorporate a higher moral standard into my life to accommodate this new ego where my own legacy is at stake.

This new set of priorities makes me examine what principles are necessary in order to develop the legacy I hope to achieve. I now have a much higher regard for guidelines based on honor, morality, and religious values. I was always cognoscente of these things before, but now it is crucial that I adhere to these principles in order to satisfy my own expectations. I have come to the conclusion that without those things, the legacy that would remain would be hollow and meaningless.

To put this into context, how many rich people die and yet have a tainted legacy because they did not dedicate themselves to others? Yes, they may have had money, power, and fame; but without honor, morality, and religious conviction, they are only considered as failures within the family of man. I will not give current examples of the people I describe, even though I can think of many, but I will pull out a classic and famous figure from the past whose name is synonymous with betrayal—Benedict Arnold.

The contribution of Benedict Arnold is only touched on in our public school system. It is too bad, too, because he had a magnificent military record while fighting for the fledgling United States of America. I think this contribution is so significant that I will list the five biggest achievements and let you decide just how important this man was.

First, when the war was just beginning, the united colonies were lacking the means to fight the British. One imbalanced military possession was cannons. The British controlled a lot of guns; the Americans had few. But there was a fort that was loaded with many sizes of canon and that was Fort Ticonderoga in upstate New York. Benedict Arnold and Ethan Allen stormed this big fortress and took possession of its stores and armory. The united colonies were going to employ these weapons at the Battle of Breed's Hill (Bunker Hill) and the siege of Boston.

Second, he engineered a second attack force for the invasion of Canada in 1775. He took what started out as a moderate amount of men (just over 1,000) through the wilderness of the Northern Colonies and Canada and arrived outside of Quebec City with a much smaller force (around 350) due to the severe obstacles and weather. Many of the men turned back, starved, or froze to death. This trek through the state of Maine is regarded as one of the most difficult and arduous tasks ever achieved in the annals of not just American history but in all of world history. Also, Arnold was shot in the leg and captured by the British during this attack in Canada and later exchanged.

Third, in the fall of 1776, it came upon Arnold to stop the invasion of New York by a British fleet led by Sir Guy Carlton. This invasion, if successful, probably would have ended the war in 1776. The Battle of Valcour Island ensued and Arnold took the dregs of society in poorly built ships and fought the best navy in the world and lost. But he did delay the invasion, led by Carlton, long enough so that they were forced to give up on the invasion and wait until the next year to try again. Most military action in that time frame avoided fighting during the winter. Originally Arnold was blamed for losing the battle but later was recognized that his heroic actions saved our country.

Fourth, when Fort Schuyler (Stanwix) was under siege in 1777, it was Arnold who rushed a force down the Mohawk Valley to turn back Barry St. Leger and defeat the second prong of the British invasion of New York of 1777. He did this using a rouse that fooled the Indian allies of the British and avoided a frontal confrontation.

And fifth, it was General Arnold who, more than anyone else was responsible for leading the battle at Freeman's Farm and securing the major victory at the Battle of Saratoga. That victory, which convinced the French to recognize our sovereignty and fight on our side, more than any other reason, was why America won the Revolutionary War. And incidentally, Arnold was once again shot in the leg, and this time it shattered.

After reading this short resume, it should be obvious that he had a major impact on the outcome of the revolutionary war. After the fact, I would have to say he earned two Purple Hearts, three Silver Stars, and, in my opinion, the Congressional Medal of Honor. I believe if he had stayed true to the cause, he would have had a chance to become the second president of the United States. What happened instead shocked this new nation right to the ground. It was so shocking, in fact, that Benedict Arnold's legacy—ultimately his very name—has become synonymous with betrayal, and still is 232 years later.

You see, people believe that Benedict Arnold was a very vain man and that he was constantly trying to prove himself. He was easily offended and was criticized quite a bit during this time because everyone was trying to move up the ladder, and in some cases, at the expense of those who showed poor judgment.

Benedict Arnold was blamed for losing the Battle of Valcour Island. He was charged with money mismanagement and court marshaled (but found not guilty), he was overlooked for contributing to the victory at Saratoga; and to add further insult to his pride, a number of foreign officers who had contributed nothing were promoted over him. I cannot accurately present how this tore at him.

He married a younger woman named Peggy Shippen who was a Tory sympathizer and many believe she hardened his heart. Arnold eventually decided to switch sides and fight the remainder of the war for the British. He tried to turn over his command at West Point in exchange for a commission in the British Army. It should also be explained that it was a very common practice at the time for soldiers to switch sides due to mistreatment or poor conditions. This was easy to do in most cases because one side wasn't really all that different from the other.

Arnold's decision carried such weight because of the notoriety he had already achieved. The details of this betrayal can be argued as his true motivations may never be known. But he did write a letter to the American people explaining why he switched sides. Maybe he would have been viewed as a hero if the British had won, but as it turned out, he died an obscure nobody in London in 1801. This is a shame for a courageous man who helped America far more than he hurt it.

But ultimately, history judges his choices and what it comes down to is that Benedict Arnold broke his oath, betrayed his country, and destroyed his own legacy. It is a perfect example of how highly we regard honor, morality, and religious conviction. I actual feel sorry for the man and his tortured ending.

I think it is fairly obvious that Benedict Arnold was not treated very well prior to his choice, but was it bad enough to commit such an egregious act? We all have free will and must respond according to our own convictions, just as Mr. Arnold did. There are only two things that I can do from this point on. First, it is to make sure that I do not share his fate. I will stand by my convictions, my honor, and my God...no matter what. And second, I would like to say, "I forgive you, Mr. Arnold."

The New Guy

THE DEVIL SAT behind his desk console and watched the video camera. He was concentrating hard on what he saw on the screen. Just then a door burst open and an ugly demon with a large red face stuck his head in the doorway.

"Master, we have a problem!"

Without turning from the screen, Satan said, "Call, me 'boss,' not 'master.' So what is it, Paymon?"

The demon entered the room wearing a black suit and tie and carrying a clipboard. He approached the desk walking briskly and then in a very formal and monotone voice replied "Sorry, boss. It looks like we have a troublemaker. He just came through admissions and an alarm went off. We think he's a runner."

The devil swiveled his chair around to a complex computer system. A password screen popped up. He entered his password, "Hotstuff666," and then he turned to the admission page. There were no alarms listed. "He's not listed. Paymon, why isn't he listed?"

The demon hadn't thought to check that. He had been trying very hard to be professional and efficient, but this made him look bad. "Sorry, mast...uhh... boss. The admissions crew is having software problems again."

The devil sighed and covered his face with his large red hand. "Why do I get all the idiots? Paymon, get me the hard file on the troublemaker...now!"

"Yes, boss!" Paymon ran out of the room.

A short time later, Satan had the file and was reading the life story of "the new guy." Every so often, the devil's eyes would rise as he read from the file. Once he finished, he closed the cover, stood up, and straightened his elegant robe. Then, with a snap of his fingers, a large puff of smoke filled the center of the room. As it dissipated, a medium-sized man appeared in its place in the middle of his office. The bewildered man spun in a circle, confused on how this unknown method of transportation worked. He was wearing a gray suit with a red tie. He wore fancy shoes, and his hair was combed back. He had the appearance of a smooth talker. He seemed like someone who had a lot of personal confidence.

The devil walked toward him as he scanned up and down. Paymon watched from a chair at the desk. He had a big grin on his face in anticipation of an entertaining show. This type of thing didn't happen very often, but when it did, Paymon always took great pleasure because he admired Satan's style. The man spied the Devil in return and did not show fear. It was strange to Paymon that they looked at each other in almost the same fashion. Their personal characteristics and demeanor seemed identical. Then the Devil shifted his weight backward and said, "Hmmm." The man finished his gaze and also concluded with a brief sound that indicated curiosity.

Satan looked at the new guy and said, "Aren't you afraid of me?"

The man looked stolid. "No. I've dealt with people like you my whole life."

The devil began to circle the man. "Really? You've met that kind of greatness just by being a campaign manager?"

The man let out a short laugh. "So you've already researched my personal file. I will take that as a compliment."

The devil sneered at the man, cleverly hiding what he really thought.

Satan had circled halfway around "the new guy" and said, "Do you know what we do with runners?" he asked. The man shook his head no as he tried to look at the devil while he was behind him. The devil smiled an evil grin. "We put them on the 'hard labor' line. It is the worst work down here!" he said.

"For how long?" asked "the new guy."

The devil laughed hard. "How long?" he repeated with a sarcastic and drawn-out burst. "You don't know anything, do you? Time doesn't matter down here... you just go on the line!"

Paymon sat motionless and studied the conversation. He continued to enjoy the exchange as he admired the devil at work. "Now why would you want to run away from here? You earned this place. I would think you'd fit in." The devil's voice was soft and exaggerated. He seemed almost to be taunting his guest. "No one wants to end up on the line; there is only one place worse." The devil now stood back in the front of the man with his hands on his hips.

The man seemed perplexed. "Who said I want to run away?"

The devil shot an angry look at Paymon who immediately shrugged his shoulders. Paymon, who functioned as Satan's top assistant, hated looking foolish to his boss. He made a mental note to torment those computer system guys right after this was over. He even decided to replace the "alarm" people. His attention quickly refocused on the exchange in front of him.

"You don't want to run away?" continued the Devil.

"No...I like it here" replied "the new guy."

The devil looked confused. "Well then...why did you set the alarms off?" he asked.

The man suddenly understood. "It wasn't because I want to run away; it was because I want to run this place."

The devil isn't normally surprised but this last statement made his head snap back. "What? That's an interesting attitude you've got there." Satan put his arm around the shoulders of the new guy and walked the man back out of the door from his office. "I know just what to do with someone like you," he said as the two of them left the room, leaving Paymon alone to plan his revenge on the support staff.

A short time later, the devil reentered the room, and Paymon's head popped up from behind the control desk. He took special interest that his boss was now alone. "What did you do with the 'campaign manager'?" he asked.

Satan smiled as he wiped his hands on a towel. "I threw him in the pit. What did you think I'd do with a troublemaker like that?"

Paymon laughed and said, "Good one, boss!"

Satan sat back down at the camera station and adjusted the channel. Then he smiled his devilish grin. "Maybe I'll let him out of there to run things when I go on vacation?" He raised his hand to his chin to consider.

Paymon looked surprised. "Boss? You never go on vacation!"

Satan turned his head and then he burst out an evil laugh. "I know—I *never* go on vacation!"

The Oath, Part 1

A LONG TIME AGO, before the dawn of man, the earth was a much simpler place. On the edge of a forest, near a very large lake, the creatures of the woods and the creatures of the plains lived out their lives. Most of the time, the animals kept to themselves. The deer lived with the deer and the bear lived with the bear, that is, most of the time.

Not long after a great flood, the animals of the forest and of the animals of the plain had to recover from the water. While their families worked at digging and building, a young fox, a tiny mouse, a small turtle, and a baby rabbit gathered in the grass near the lake. The four of them played out in the open while a little cardinal watched them from a large oak tree.

"Watch out for the great owl!" warned the cardinal. The five new friends would quickly look at the sky and then go back to playing. The little cardinal spent most of his time singing in the tree while keeping watch. Their parents were busy and so the young ones took this time to explore their small part of the world.

The turtle would carry the mouse and the little fox would jump over them. The rabbit would leap as high as he could as the cardinal would fly by. They would hide and jump, laugh and run until they were so tired that they had to rest. They would go to the lake, get a drink of water, and then sleep under the large oak tree, hiding from the heat of the sun.

Then one afternoon, while they played in the field, the cardinal cried out, "The owl! The owl!" The four friends ran under the oak as fast as they could. The turtle, naturally, was last. The owl circled the field, staring with his great eyesight. The five of them stayed hidden and motionless under the protection of the large oak tree until the great bird flew away. The little animals were afraid to move. Then the cardinal said, "He's gone…we're safe!" They were all relieved.

The little rabbit motioned for them to come together. "You, too, cardinal!" said the rabbit. They gathered in a small circle. "I propose that we always stay friends, and if any of us should ever need help, we do whatever we can to be there." As the grass swayed in the sun, the five little friends swore an oath that day under the branches of the large oak tree.

The years went by and the little creatures grew up and went their own ways. The fox had a family and hunted on the far side of the forest. The turtle had little ones of his own, as he moved to the other side of the lake. The rabbit now lived across the plain and was part of a large warren. The cardinal had a summer nest and a family in the very same oak tree. And the mouse was so small and so hard to keep track of that no one was sure where he lived, but the cardinal would see him from time to time.

They were living their lives and tending to the things grown-ups attend to, and the oath of their childhood became a distant memory. It is easy to forget things as time goes by, but some things cannot be forgotten.

The fox was busy looking for dinner. He stayed crouched in the shade as the long blades of summer grass swayed back and forth. He slowly prepared to pounce on his prey. Then, just as he was about to spring forward, the little mouse emerged from the foliage. "Mouse, is that you?" asked the fox. He nodded yes. "You should be more careful…I could have eaten you!" The little mouse trembled and wanted to speak. His voice was so soft and shaky that the fox had to lean close. "What's wrong?" he asked.

"Weeee, weeee…we have a problem," he said. "The rabbit has been taken away by the great owl."

The fox stood there thinking of what that must feel like. *Poor rabbit,* thought the fox, *but what does that have to do with me? He surely must be dead…and if he isn't, he soon will be.*

The mouse tried to speak, but he was still shaking. Then he took a deep breath and tried again. "The turtle...heeee...heeee...wants us to meet at the oak tree."

The fox stepped back. "The turtle?" he said. "What for?"

The mouse gathered the energy to speak loudly so the fox could hear him plainly, and in his shaky voice, he said, "The oath!"

The fox was stunned. When he woke up this morning, he never would have guessed things would turn out like this...but here it was. It was years later and the oath of his childhood was being called upon. The very thought of it was silly, but an oath is an oath. The fox lay down and the mouse climbed on his back. "Hang on!" he said. He paced himself and he trotted all the way back to the large oak tree.

When he arrived, the cardinal and the turtle were sitting under the tree. The fox let the mouse down and the four of them stared at each other. They had not been together since that summer they swore the oath.

The turtle began. "We have to help the rabbit! The owl snatched him up early this morning. And that fierce bird has two young ones, I've been told. Right now they sleep. They won't wake for dinner until this evening."

The fox shook his head. "That means we have less than half a day to go get him. The owl lives on the other end of the lake high on the mountainside. How could we get there in time?" asked the fox. The other three looked at him blankly.

"We have to save him," stated the cardinal.

"I'm not much for plans," said the turtle, "but I can swim across the lake."

"I'm not much for plans either," said the cardinal, "but I can fly up that mountain."

"I'm surely not much for plans," said the mouse in his squeaky voice, "but I am small and I can chew."

The fox shook his head up and down and smiled. "Well, I can run…and I am good at plans. Now, here's what we're going to do…" said the fox. The animals leaned in close.

The fox carried the turtle and the mouse all the way to the shortest part of the lake. He ran as fast as he could while the cardinal flew behind him. And when they arrived on the shore, the turtle and the mouse got down. The animals looked around and noticed that a fog was rolling in across the lake as the sun was getting low in the sky. The turtle waited, and the mouse and the cardinal got on his back. The turtle couldn't run well at all, but he sure could swim. Out into the lake he went toward the mountain on the other side. "Good luck," yelled the fox as the turtle, the cardinal, and the mouse disappeared into the rolling mist.

The turtle finally reached the far shore just as the sun was setting. The mouse ran over to the cliff on the side of the mountain and looked up. The mountain was enormous compared to the little rodent, and the mouse was afraid. "Have courage!" yelled the turtle. The cardinal picked up the mouse and flew up the side of the mountain toward the owl's nest. "Good luck!" shouted the turtle as his two old friends disappeared from sight. The cardinal arrived at the underside of the owl's nest just as the light began to fade in the sky. They only had moments before the baby owls would awaken.

"Hurry, mouse," he whispered. The mouse began to chew into the bottom of the nest as fast as he could. Soon he made a hole big enough to climb through. He poked his head into the opening and there, not five feet away, was the rabbit. The mouse ran over and sat on his neck. "Wake up, rabbit" he whispered in his ear.

The rabbit stirred and his eyes slowly opened. "Mouse? Is that you? Am I dead?" he asked.

"You will be in just a minute of you don't do exactly what I say." The baby owls were walking toward them. Their eyes were yellow and cold. The rabbit trembled with fear.

"What do I do?"

The mouse grabbed a hold of the rabbit's fur. "Jump!" said the mouse.

"Jump?" said the rabbit. "Are you crazy?"

The mouse smiled. "I must be," he said. "Jumping is what rabbits do, isn't it? Trust me!"

The rabbit jumped out of the nest just as the baby owls lunged forward. The young birds had just missed out on breakfast. The rabbit fell out of the nest and plummeted down the side of the mountain with the mouse clinging to his back. The rabbit was sure he was going to die.

The cardinal swooped in through the twilight and grabbed the rabbit by the neck. He flapped and flapped to try to stop their descent, but it was too much weight for one cardinal. So he did the only thing left that he could think of. He pulled the rabbit and the mouse out over the lake while they fell. He continued to try to flap to slow them down, but he soon became exhausted. The three of them crashed into the water.

The turtle swam to them as fast as he could. It wasn't long before the mouse, the cardinal and the rabbit were on the turtle's back heading across the lake. All three were unconscious, but the turtle was pretty sure that they were all breathing.

The turtle arrived on the shore a little ways to the north of where he started. He rolled his three friends onto the beach. He nudged them and one by one they awoke. The rabbit was the last one to awaken, and just when he did and his eyes began to focus, a look of fear crossed his dazed face. The owl stood there with his wife and his two young ones. They began to slowly walk toward them. "So you thought you could get away? I am the great owl!" he said as he spread his wings. "I do not lose my prey!" he boasted.

Just then through the fog came a yip. The fox emerged from the mist. The owls stopped their approach and stared at the fox. "You will be the first one we take!" said the owl. "I don't think so!" said the fox. Suddenly one wolf after another leapt from the fog and surrounded the owls. The owls were completely encircled. "I'd like you to meet my cousins!" said the fox. The wolves growled at the four birds.

Without saying another word, the owls quickly flew into the night sky and disappeared. The fox turned to his friends. "Welcome back, rabbit!" The rabbit smiled but he wasn't too happy with the way the wolves were looking at him. The fox chuckled. "They're joking!" and with that, the wolves laughed. One by one they greeted the rabbit as they disappeared back into the mist.

Early the next morning, the turtle, the rabbit, the cardinal, the mouse, and the fox sat under the large oak tree. They rested there together and enjoyed the peacefulness of the morning. The cardinal started to sing while the mouse sat on the turtle's back and the rabbit curled up next to the fox. It was so many years ago that they played together as kids. The oak tree and the field was still the same, but everything seemed smaller to them. And now they were grown up with families of their own. The days of their youth were just distant memories, but they never forgot their friendship. And they never forgot their oath.

The Quality of Mercy

HOW DO WE judge ourselves? Do you look in the mirror every now and then and ask: "Who am I?" Or maybe we ask: "Did I really do that?" Or even worse, "Man, I wish that never happened!" I'm sure sometimes it goes the other way too. Sometimes we look in the mirror and we are genuinely proud of ourselves. Those moments help us to "strut." They affect the way we act and it gives us a certain kind of "glow."

I am going to speak of what I believe is the most important quality that a human being can exhibit. It is the quality of mercy. I've said this for years: "It is the one thing that separates us from the animals." I hope you don't mind that I just quoted myself. I believe the best examples of mercy are found in the history books.

Most people don't think too much about history. Most young people will say, "History is boring!" But I believe the key to our future is there. Every event that we experience, where we think it's never happened before, is already recorded in history somewhere. And so the lesson in this story comes from history. As this story unfolds, try to ask yourself: "What would I have done?"

In the late fall of 1862, America was deep into the Civil War. The North was desperate for a victory and the southern army was winning battle after battle. The North had more men and more equipment, but the South had better generals.

In December of that year, a desperate Federal Army decided it needed to attack the entrenched southern army in Fredericksburg, Virginia. The northern army was going to have to cross a large depressed area and then ascend uphill to a wall to get to the rebel lines. On December 13, 1862, the northern armies attempted one of the worst conceived plans in North American military history.

In one particular area, a place known as Marye's Heights, some 8,000 union soldiers were shot, and many of them lay wounded in the area between the Northern and Southern lines as the day came to a close with the setting of the sun. Thousands of soldiers cried out in agony while soldiers from both sides could only sit and listen.

It was very dangerous to travel in that area between as soldiers from either side would shoot at anything that moved in the dark. Try to imagine the torture on a sound mind trying to guard your area while having to listen to that ghastly and ghostly noise.

Those who were injured suffered more than just battle wounds. They were also cold and dehydrated. They cried out for home, for loved ones, and for life itself. It is at this point that one man took it upon himself to change things.

Sergeant Richard Kirkland of South Carolina asked for and was reluctantly granted permission to bring water and blankets to the men trapped in that "no man's land." He was told he could not bring a white flag or any other kind of emblem. This added to the danger, but it wasn't going to stop him. So he gathered up as many canteens and blankets as he could carry and he went out to bring aid and comfort to men who were suffering. Remember that most of those wounded and dying men were from the North.

He knew that it was likely he was going to get shot. He knew that once one side fired, the other side would fire back and the effect would be murderous. But in his own words, "I'll take my chances," he said as he climbed over the wall and down the hill. To his surprise, no one fired. Instead, cheers went up from both sides in the starlight. Sergeant Kirkland spent the next couple of hours making several trips back and forth. He continued to go to wherever a man cried for water until everyone had a drink.

Sergeant Kirkland was given the nickname "The Angel of Marye's Heights." A statue now stands in his honor at Fredericksburg, Virginia. Sergeant Kirkland was more than just war hero; he was a hero for all humanity. Later the next year he proved his mortality as he was killed in this war at the Battle of Chickamauga. It was a very unceremonious death for a man who deserved more.

I once read a quote a long time ago from a person that I've misplaced that said: "It is important in our darkest times to remember to show mercy." It is one thing to show mercy, it is another thing to risk your life doing it—and Sergeant Kirkland did both. He is a hero of mine. And if I am ever as unfortunate to find myself in that kind of situation, I hope I would be capable to do the same thing…regardless of the risks to my own personal safety.

The Reality of Reality

FROM THE MOMENT we are born until the last instant of our lives, we go through a process that starts with nothing and ends with nothing. Everything in between those two events is a journey that can lead us in almost any direction. We fill in that journey with one personal experience after another. Hopefully, as we get older, we build up knowledge and experience to become wiser than we were in our youth. Some of our experiences give us great insight. Other things haunt us for great periods of time as we try to come to terms with the complexity of the event. Some things affect us right to the core of our being and change our path altogether. Other things bounce off and become avenues that we will not pursue. Ultimately we become a type of "quilt" of our experiences. Every one of us has a "different pattern" to our "quilts." And some of us actually have enough insight to see these different patterns and respect them.

Every time we experience something new, our list of experiences grows larger. Another patch is added to our "quilt." It has always bothered me to know that when we die, that lifetime of experiences is lost, like the jokes known by Henny Youngman or the war stories of a World War II veteran. I have always wondered how much of my mother was lost forever when she passed on.

The point of this story, however, isn't to lament death and the information that is lost. It is to explain how one very important piece of information, one square of my "quilt," has helped me to adjust to most every situation in life.

In order to live in society, it is important to understand what it is that motivates people and what is important to them. When you understand that, you will be much more successful in relationships of every kind. I learned that at a young age. I also knew that these motivations change based on where you are. Different cultures have different priorities. And I felt that the best way to learn these priorities was to study the different religions around the world.

This was a very sound plan, and as a student of human nature, it was a very good place to begin. But what I found out later in life was that it was a place to start but not the place to end. You see, there is one aspect to human nature that supersedes all other tendencies, and I learned it one day, as clear as could be, by a failed business transaction.

The day of my enlightenment began as a repairman for a large copier company. I was called to an account because one of our machines was not working well. The customer in question was a high school office and their complaint was that their copier was jamming far too often.

I responded to the call in a timely manner and began by inspecting the condition of the machine. I checked the electronic error log and then made note of the call history. I subsequently filled the machine with paper and began to test how well it worked. I ran somewhere between 600 to 800 copies, and the machine worked very well. I then made a calculation based on the error log that the customer had only two jams in the last 1000 copies. Our criterion was that anything less than three jams per thousand was considered a well-functioning machine. The reason for some jams can be blamed on poor paper quality. Sometimes humidity can even cause a machine to jam, and it was the middle of summer.

I concluded the service call by assuring the customer that I had tested the machine and that it was working within specifications. I then left the account and went on with my work schedule. That high school and that machine did not call back in, so I assumed it was a successful service visit. This could not have been further from the truth.

About a month later, we were having a service meeting. My "team" assembled in our normal meeting room and we began to review our performance over the last month or so. We began to discuss sales activity when we noticed that we had lost the account at the high school I had visited a month earlier. We questioned the salesman about this information, and he explained that there was nothing he could do.

The customer was convinced that they had a poor-performing machine and wanted nothing more to do with our company. I explained to the group that they actually had a pretty-good-running copier and that they misunderstood what constituted a poor-performing machine. The customer obviously wanted something that ran more like a modern TV set (those things rarely break, and when they do people just buy a new one). The customer just didn't understand that a copier is not a TV set.

The salesman looked at me and said, "What difference does that make? The reality of the situation is that we lost a machine because the customer *thought* they had a poor-performing machine. It isn't how the copier runs; it's how the customer *thinks* it runs." It suddenly became crystal clear in my mind. The customer's perception is what mattered here.

I suddenly realized that I needed to fix the customer's perception, not the customer's machine. Obviously it was too late in this situation but the lesson had been learned. I stewed about it for a while. This was a loss that did not have to happen. I lost a good-running machine because I misunderstood what was happening in that office. But that isn't the end of the issue.

We developed a short questionnaire to try to identify customers who had "perception" issues. We thought that if we could address misconceptions, we could increase customer satisfaction and increase sales. It was a great idea that prevented similar situations from becoming an unfortunate reality. The more I thought about it, the more I realized how I not only misunderstood human nature but also how ignorant I was of the magnitude of the problem. The truth here is that this philosophical ideal pervades everything where people are involved.

I could now see the bigger picture of life. Perception is reality. Not just with copiers and office accounts, but with everything. It determines our satisfaction with all the functions of society. It dictates who wins the big court cases. It decides whether or not you get that new job, or how well a movie does at the box office. Perception really is what drives everything.

I think back to all the time I spent in a classroom. I remember countless hours behind a chalkboard. I went from kindergarten to college. I've taken religious, military, and educational classes of every sort, and the most important philosophical life lesson that there is to learn, I learned at a failed copier service call.

And now I know that if you want to understand people, you not only have to understand their religion, their culture, and the path that they have taken, but you also have to take into account their perception. And once you do that, things will become a lot easier to understand. It is also important to realize that some mistakes can lead you to a better approach. And the quilt that is my life became stronger and more complete by experiencing that mistake.

The Sailor and the Witch

THE MORNING SKY was red, and yet it was welcomed. The ocean crashed into the large rocks of the coast as the tide began to recede. The lighthouse stood there like a soldier guarding his post. The tower shined on its western side as the red sunlight rose over the sea. The spray from the ocean covered the rocks, and the mist it created floated up and over the short cliffs.

The sun ended the previous night and all of nature seemed to exhale in relief. Every sailor knew that the red sky was an indication of foul weather to come. But the night before had finally ended and the sky had cleared. Many would swear that it had been unnaturally long, but fear will do that to the mind. Now it was just a memory that would be retold around campfires for years to come.

The wind was gone now but it had been howling loudly for most of the night. The town that sat a few miles away could hear the wind, the rain, and the ocean, and later many would swear that they heard the screams. Not many villagers would venture outside today. Fear can be spread like the flu. It starts with a few and can affect anyone it touches.

A schooner was trapped in a gale the night before during a sudden squall. The small shipping crew saw the lighthouse and heard the ocean slamming on the rocks but was unable to turn away. The six men on board fought with the rigging but had not been prepared for the sudden storm. It came upon them so quickly that they were convinced there was an evil behind it.

Their sails were catching a light breeze during the night and they were on their way home. Suddenly, the storm arose and before the small crew could change the rigging, the sound of wood cracking and water rushing in could be heard. The lighthouse was quickly upon them and they knew their ship and their fish were lost.

Only three of them managed to make it to shore. The frame and hull of the ship was heard smashing into the rocks while they fought to breathe in the cold saltwater. The three sailors lay on the beach in the driving rain a short time later. Exhaustion forced them to lay there with the cold water slapping at them. Soon the rain turned to hail and the force of the small ice pelted them while they recovered face down in the sand.

They were overcome with sadness and relief at the same time, but those emotions would soon be replaced with another. They were not aware that they were very close to the stream that ran from the hollow of the witch.

Another hour later saw the three men stagger off the beach looking for shelter. The terrain of the land led them up and over a small cliff and then through the woods. The rain was not as fierce under the cover of the autumn canopy that trembled and shook in the wind. There was nothing to guide them as they stumbled through the undergrowth and the darkness.

Then a light could be seen in the distance on the far side of the hollow. It appeared menacing despite the poor weather conditions. There was a large tree that had fallen and was propped up on crumpled branches. It seemed like a natural fence that separated the dense part of the woods to the small field and structure below. By the time the fallen tree was reached, only two sailors leaned over it to study the view down beneath them.

Sounds could be heard through the wind and the rain. Branches were snapping and a figure could be seen dancing across the field. It seemed to float with an unnatural motion as if the figure barely made contact with the ground. Its arms were outstretched before it as it slowly spun while it undulated up and down. Then suddenly its mannerisms changed. It began to move quickly in a zigzag pattern as if it was searching for something. The two sailors squinted to focus in the darkness as a second figure appeared through the branches on the far side of the field. The darkness, the weather, and the distance made it difficult to be certain, but the two men suddenly found themselves captured by fear at the sight of their shipmate exposed to the approaching apparition.

Suddenly the floating figure straightened its course like an angry hornet and shot forward at an unnatural speed. It crashed through the branches in the direction of their confused and lost shipmate. Almost instantly, a scream burst forth that filled the hollow and the surrounding hills. The two remaining sailors ran back into the woods the way they came. The scream seemed to chase them as they fled into the darkness. They ran with an intensity that exceeded their own safety in the darkness of the woods.

Later that night, the two men were found in the lighthouse. One had a large gash on his head. He was spread out on the floor in a small puddle of dried blood. He had been dead for a couple of hours. His body was cold to the touch. The second man was carried back into the village while the wind and the rain seemed to fight off the rising of the sun.

A short time later, the lone surviving sailor was awake and sitting by a fireplace. The tavern wasn't normally open at this time in the early morning but this morning was not normal. He was given some warm soup which he held but refused to drink. He muttered his story while he rocked back and forth. The villagers that were there were convinced something terrible had happened, but where reality began and imagination ended was hard to say. The only thing that was certain at that moment was that the fear of the unknown began to spread through the town.

None of the other sailors were ever found. Most of the wreckage from the schooner was pulled back out to sea during the storm. The only survivor died the next day in his sleep. The doctor said it was from shock. The villagers believed it was the witch who was thought to torture and curse those who trespass.

The bodies of the two sailors that were accounted for were buried in the cemetery, but no one attended. The villagers made no attempt to find out who they were. They were buried in two unmarked graves with just wooden crosses to protect them.

Yes, the storm from the previous night was over. The morning sky was beautiful and foreboding. The villagers whispered amongst themselves that the color of the horizon resembled blood in a slaughterhouse. It warned everyone that the weather would be violent by nightfall, and yet the red ominous morning was welcomed.

The Sand

THE DESERT IS a lonely place. There is a light breeze today. The sand travels across the dunes and whips out into the air before falling back to the earth. There is a stillness which accompanies the wind. There are no animals to see as they all hide in the shade of what few rocks there are. There are only a small number of inhabitants in this most inhospitable region and they wisely sleep during the heat of the day.

Only those with foolish intentions venture out into this part of the desert. There is no water for miles. There are few places to seek refuge and the heat bears down with an unforgiving intensity. There are no clouds and the sun is relentless. The wind blows, and to the naked eye the moving sand is the only thing that gives it away.

There are no trees to bend, no leaves to shake, and no branches to sway. There is no grass or any other vegetation as far as the eye can see. There is only wave after wave of sand, and the sand is hiding its secrets. It has a past and a future. It was there yesterday and it will be there tomorrow. It ages but it doesn't get old.

There are no birds in the sky to look upon. Their friendly and hypnotic effects are absent. Birds are like accidents on the highway. They force you to look, to take notice. They say "Here I am! Look at me fly!" but they are not there.

If a guest were to stare at the desert long enough, one would see a pattern emerge. The wind and the sand—blowing, pulsating, rising and falling—would begin to appear to make sense. It has its own personality—a plan, a will. It is constant and unyielding like the tides of the ocean or the rain that partners with a typhoon.

There are three colors and three colors alone. There is the blue of the sky, the light-brown sand, and the yellow of the sun. It is easy to see how a prolonged trip in this arena could drive a man mad. There is nothing to navigate by—no landmarks, no hills, no structures, just sand. It seems odd to think that one could get lost where so little exists. But that is the one great trap of the desert.

There is a sound that can be heard but it also has the characteristics of an illusion. The wind will rise in the ear and then slowly die away. It will repeat this rhythm over and over until the person listening forgets that it's even there. Your mind will drown it out like background music while you sleep. But every once in a while there is a whistle that accompanies the force and it reminds you of where you are.

Clothing is the biggest contradiction of all. It seems that the most reasonable approach would be to wear nothing, but the sun is far too aggressive for that. Thick clothing might bring protection from the sand, but that, too, would be a mistake. A light robe is the most practical response, and a white robe is the coolest as the sun is reflected rather than absorbed.

Very few would venture out into a place such as this. This is not the kind of environment for a novice. The desert can kill. It does so slowly and without remorse. It attacks the brain as it dehydrates its victims into a slow delirium. Reality becomes confused and distorted, and the likelihood of escaping the clutches of this beast decrease constantly with the sun.

One would have to question the motivation of a stranger here. This is not a place that people come to live, but rather it is a warm and relentless tomb. To the voyeur, there is nothing to be gained by being here. There is nothing to accomplish. There is very little to learn. The effects are stifling, and those who know the desert bear the mark.

Close your eyes for a moment and see it in your mind. Try to imagine what it looks like. Can you see it? Can you feel its warmth? Can you hear the wind? Did you notice there is nothing to smell and nothing to taste? Your body is suddenly stifled by the blast of dry hot air that feels like an open oven door.

The sand shines and shimmers in wave after wave of glistening crystals. The dunes roll along. They rise and fall. The lack of moisture and the intensity of the sun burn and scorch anything that is not sand. The air bends into illusion as the warm air creates a distortion to those who try to look into the distance. The mirage of water is created and leads those who need it the most to find out that they are victims of the desert as it is playing a very cruel trick.

There is nothing notable to record. No sound that is worth replaying. No video that is worth passing along. There is no painting worth the cost. No photograph that is worth framing. One could spend a month staring out into the desert with nothing to report, nothing to retell, and nothing to recapture.

But look close and you will see the symmetry, the structure, the balance. Thomas Aquinas and his fifth proof stands out here (look it up). It is something that you could easily miss as the vast majority of people are encumbered by other things. It is something that you can't explain, but rather something that you "feel." A person devoid of sensitivity would not see it. A logical man will refute it. Every laboratory in the world would say that there is no proof, but I tell you there is something there. Something easily overlooked, something more. There, in the most remote place on earth, is the face of God.

The Soldier

THE TEMPERATURE WAS warm and the ocean melodically pulsated on the beach like it had for thousands of years. The sun shone down on a nearly cloudless day as a light breeze cooled the sand and the rocky terrain further inland. From one perspective, the beach looked a lot like it had through the ages, but from another perspective, this day was anything but calm and peaceful.

The soldiers who had run across the beach were now crawling forward, trying to avoid the constant stream of bullets and projectiles that flew overhead. The men, wearing full battle gear, were hot, wet, dirty, and tired.

Their progress was slow and the sounds and smells of battle stung their ears and noses.

Smoke blew across the beach from each explosion, and the effect of this battle on the soldiers who slowly made their way inland would stay with the participants their whole lives. It is difficult to accurately describe the horror and the fear experienced in these situations. The soldiers tried not to dwell on the thought of getting killed, but every now and again a fellow soldier would go down. Sometimes they died outright. Sometimes they had treatable injuries and sometimes it was only a matter of when they died. It is one thing to know some might die, it is something else entirely to see a friend of yours whom you were talking to only moments ago die in horrible agony.

A lone soldier made his way through the sand to the far left of the attack. He sensed a clear path to the rocks ahead and the illusion of safety. He crawled through the sand in a slight depression and was drawing near to the end of the beach. Beads of sweat rolled down his nose and clung there momentarily. They mixed with the dirt on his face before falling to the ground. This soldier was at battle with his own fear. He did not want to be a statistic. Just a few more feet and he would be off the beach. The sounds of mortar fire and a machine gun nest filled his head as he inched ever closer.

Then, just as he started to believe he might make it, a deafening concussion left him lying face up and disoriented in the sand. He shook his head slightly as he tried to understand what it was that had just happened. A mortar had exploded next to him and the effects had left him stunned. As he looked up above and took deep breaths, he could see bullets sailing by overhead making the shining blue sky appear gray.

The humming in his ears began to clear, and he suddenly became aware of numbness in the lower half of his body. He tried to sit straight but he could only lift himself up a short ways. As he looked down at his legs, a sudden nausea hit him at the realization that he had been cut open from the hip to the knee on the left side of his body. His blood was soaking into the sand. His helmet had rolled off his head, and his rifle lay by his side, peacefully, quietly, and partially covered.

The soldier now had to consider that his life was over. He quickly realized all the things that were still left to do that he would never get to. He thought of how sad his mother and father were going to be. *This is going to kill her...I'm sorry, Mom!* he thought. He had wanted to see Europe. He wondered if he would have ever had a family of his own, and he thought about his dog.

There is a reason that young people make the best soldiers. They are the most malleable and the easiest to train. They think they are indestructible and they are in their peak physical state. But the sad side is that they have lived so little. The death of a young soldier is a shame. Part of me thinks that old soldiers should be the ones to die on a beach in the middle of nowhere.

The soldier's numbness was starting to go away and the pain from his injuries was making him dizzy. He was sure that he didn't have long. He would bleed to death before anyone found him. He wanted to sit up to try to stop the bleeding, but the pain and the sand prevented him.

He tried to calm his breathing as he lay back down flat on the soft earth. He could feel a few stray rocks underneath him while he looked up at the sky. He suddenly remembered his varsity football coach telling him he would never amount to anything, and it was just because he missed two practices. How silly any of that seemed now as the smoke and the bullets went by.

He started to take slower deep breaths as it seemed to ease the terrible pain that he felt. He closed his eyes thinking that he would never reopen them. He could hear the sounds of screaming a distance away. He could feel his head pound with each beat of his heart. He was accepting his death.

Just then a soldier with a red cross on his arm band came sliding to a stop by his side. He dropped his bag and began to rip a cloth into a bandage. The last words he heard on that beach were "I got you! I got you!"

I would like to thank all of the men and women, soldiers and sailors who have fought, suffered, and given of themselves so that my family and I can enjoy peace and freedom. It is easy to overlook this sacrifice sometimes. So here it is: "Thank you!"

The Sounds at the Tire Swing, Part 1

THE STREAM IN the back of Opie's house was a very popular site during the summer. It would draw children from all over the area. It was a great place to go for a swim. The current was deep and slow just past a big bend, and the children from years past had put up a tire swing on the big maple tree that hung over the water. This setting—the stream, the tire swing, the trees—could very well have been a picture postcard photo or a painting of "Americana." And Opie never once complained of the path that was worn out in his yard where the children cut through to get there.

The sounds of laughter and splashing could be heard from Opie's window during the heat of a summer's day. And often, on a warm summer night, the sound and smell of a campfire and older kids enjoying life could be heard in his bedroom. Opie sometimes felt lonely in the winter, spring, and fall, but never in the summer.

Opie was a retired policeman who had spent thirty years on the police force. He was a sixty-five-year-old widower who now maintained his house by himself. He had two dogs who shared his life, but he was alone for the most part. He had two children who were in their thirties, but both of them had moved to opposite ends of the country, and he only saw them on major holidays.

Opie did a good job of keeping his yard neat. He kept the grass short and the lawn raked. It was the inside of his house he hated to clean. He had a fence on the left side of his yard but nothing obstructed the right side at all. That is why the shortcut through his yard to the stream became so popular. His property ended a couple of hundred yards before the tire swing, but the neighboring children still referred to the swimming area as "Opie's."

Opie's dogs would bark every now and then when someone would cut through his yard, but he never had a problem worth worrying about. Both of his dogs were mixed breeds and they both weighed about seventy pounds. They were both middle-aged as dogs go, and both had a very friendly temperament. Most of the time, the dogs would end up down at the stream with the kids. There were many summer days when they would come home wet from swimming. Opie was never sure if it was by their choice or by the choice of the kids.

Sometimes on warm summer evenings, Opie would take "Katie" and "Kelly," his two dogs, down to the stream and check on the children enjoying the warm weather. All the kids knew "officer" Opie. The older kids were mostly respectful and the younger kids seemed to treat him as a father figure. His two dogs would join right in, and he would get greeted warmly by the children he knew the best. Little Milo would always try to get a hug, and his older sister, Cheryl Lynn, would always stand in front of him with a big smile, and she wouldn't go away until he said hi. He never knew what was going on in the mind of a fifteen-year-old girl.

Friday night came and the temperature climbed into the 90s. Opie was content to stay inside with the air conditioner. He periodically would look outside his window to see who was taking the "shortcut." He attributed his curiosity to his lifelong occupation as a policeman. Everything seemed like a normal summer day until dusk came. He saw a group of five older teenage boys cross his yard on the way to the stream. He only recognized two of them. One was the Roberts boy whom he knew quite well. The other was a troubled kid whom he only knew as "Tony." He lived in the trailer park on the far south side of town. Opie thought it was bad news to see the Roberts boy hanging around with Tony. He immediately figured that the other three boys must be from the neighboring town to the south and must be associated with the trailer park. Opie thought nothing more about it as he got caught up in a crime drama on TV.

Later the night, Opie was awoken by a powerful thunderstorm. He could feel Katie and Kelly pacing in his bedroom. There would be a crash of thunder, and the dogs would be pressed right up to his mattress. Opie decided to get up and wait out the storm with the dogs. He looked out of the window just as a bolt of lightning lit up the sky and temporarily gave the impression of daylight. It was 4 a.m. when Opie turned on the weather channel. He looked at the radar and decided he had a half an hour before it would pass. He made a cup of coffee and patted his canine companions as he slid into his chair and turned the channel to see what might be on at this odd time in the morning.

He stopped on the local news channel just as a picture of a missing boy came up on the screen. The picture looked a lot like the Roberts boy. He turned the sound up. His "police" experience told him that something was wrong. He wrote the number down for "anyone with information call..." The wind and the rain were starting to die down outside, and Opie turned the piece of paper over and over in his hand. He thought about checking out the stream before he called the number.

Just then a loud howl filled the air. A cold chill went down his neck as he quickly looked at his two dogs to determine who to blame. He looked at Katie and Kelly as the two animals were both glued to the side of his chair. Neither one of them had opened their mouths. Opie suddenly realized that the loud primeval noise must have come from outside. It was very strange that it should be so loud over the distant thunder and through the walls of his living room. He abruptly decided to go investigate the stream down by the tire swing before calling the phone number.

He considered waiting for the sun to come up. In another hour, the sky should be lighter and calmer, but he knew from experience that time in regard to a missing person was the most critical factor. He quickly got dressed, put on a raincoat, and got his big flashlight from his closet. He decided to leave his dogs inside just in case another stray was running around outside in the darkness. Opie then did something that surprised even himself. He got his revolver out of his desk. He made sure it was loaded and he put it in his pocket.

Opie walked through the darkness as a spattering of rain and wind bounced off of his raincoat. He went over the slight hill at the end of his yard and crossed the short distance to the stream. The rain had turned most of the dirt to mud as he slowly went down the embankment toward the water, being extra careful not to slip on the slanted ground. His flashlight showed that a number of little feet and bigger feet had been back and forth along the soft ground of the bank of the stream. He shined his light on the lonely tire swing as it swung in a wide loop from the large maple tree. The shadow of the tire swing created an almost ghostly image of a second swing on the far shore of the stream. Opie walked halfway down the stream and suddenly questioned the purpose of this trip. *There is nothing to see out here...I should go back in and call,* he thought.

Right at that moment, his flashlight showed something else in the soft mud intermingled with the footprints. It appeared to be tracks of a large dog mixed in and on top of the footprints. Opie was unsure of which ones were laid there first as his mind raced with possibilities. He could tell by the marks that the animal had been running by the way they were dug into the ground. He momentarily thought it meant nothing, but then his police instincts reminded him that something wasn't making sense.

Then in a large flash of lightning and a large boom of thunder, Opie turned to see a very large dog on the hill. He quickly switched hands with the flashlight to get his revolver out of his pocket. The rain and the wind were making things much more complicated than he wanted it to be. By the time he had the weapon ready and the flashlight pointed, the only thing that remained was a vacated hill.

Opie trudged back home through the mud and the rain at a quick pace. He was uncomfortable with all of this. He quickly removed his wet raingear as he entered the house. He found Katie and Kelly hiding in the corner of his living room. A cold chill went up his spine as he had never seen his dogs act this way. He picked up the piece of paper with the phone number on it and lifted the phone to his ear. He was just about to dial the number when he noticed that the number of missing boys in the news story on the television had grown. The pictures on the television were now comprised of four photographs. Two of the young men Opie didn't recognize, but one of them was the Roberts boy. And there was no mistaking that the fourth boy was the troubled kid, "Tony."

The former police officer stood there with mouth open. He seemed frozen in place as his mind raced. He was suddenly broken from the trance by a very loud and unnatural howl. It seemed to fill the air in his living room as if it originated right in front of him. It ran loud and long while Opie stared at Katie and Kelly pinned in the corner of the living room shivering in fear.

The retired police officer turned and looked out of his window toward the hill leading to the tire swing down by the stream. Just then a bolt of lightning lit up the sky and the outline of the wolf stood on the top of the hill. The animal leaned back its head and let out another long howl toward the broken cloud cover which exposed the full moon on the horizon as it prepared to set.

The tire swing at the stream, which had always been the site of children's laughter, was now a place of blood and death. It was in possession of the beast.

What Didn't Happen

I'VE NOTICED THAT as I've gotten older, time seems to pass by quicker than it used to. I recently had another birthday, and now I have to consider myself on the downward side of the hill. Now that I'm older, I've come to realize that there is a perspective I never considered when I was young. It isn't because I lack intelligence or education; it is because this perspective is not a normal function of the human condition, and only a large amount of life experience allows this perspective to develop.

The perspective that I am referring to is judging the effect of the things that have not happened. Obviously the human mind is very good with inductive reasoning.

Dogs, birds, and just about every animal can adapt to inductive reasoning. That's where you drop a ball twenty times and it bounces every time. When you drop it for the twenty-first time, you know it's going to bounce—that is inductive reasoning.

Deductive reasoning is when you put things together by calculation. Let's say I have a measuring cup that will hold two cups of water and my recipe calls for two and one-half cups of water. So I add two cups of water, and then I put one-half cup in and add that. I deduced how to solve that little problem. So far, only humanity has that mental capacity on this planet.

Deductive reasoning has so many avenues, so many applications, and it can overwhelm anyone when things get complicated. And using this type of reasoning in an attempt to foresee events which could have occurred but didn't are potentially endless. One could spend all day thinking about things that didn't happen. My point on this topic is specific, however. Throughout history, there have been many significant moments of things that have happened. But there are also a number of very significant things that didn't happen.

For instance, George W. Bush was president during the 9/11 attacks. And whether or not you think he responded correctly, one inescapable truth is evident, and that is that there was not another attack when we were most vulnerable. Yet, it is hard to give credit to someone for something that didn't happen.

Another example is that when Dwight D. Eisenhower was president, he decided that nuclear weapons, even the small strategic ones, would not be used in battle. He established this precedent and luckily, every subsequent ruler with control of these weapons has followed his direction. And yet, President Eisenhower does not get acknowledged very often for preventing devastation because it has not occurred.

This brings me to the point of this issue. I believe there is one man in American history, more than any other, who may have influenced the direction of our nation, and subsequently the path of the world. His contribution to American history is overlooked, because the outcome is something that didn't happen.

The man I speak of isn't Washington, Lincoln, Franklin, or Roosevelt. It isn't Hamilton, Edison, Patton, or Truman. This hero is a man who lost a war. It is a man who is probably the most beloved general in American history and also a man who led a failed revolution. The man I speak of is Robert E. Lee, the Civil War general from Virginia.

Robert E. Lee fought a masterful war against the North. He won battle after battle even though his adversary constantly had more men, more food, more guns, a naval blockade, and a much bigger war chest. After four years of fighting, Ulysses S. Grant finally wore him down to the point where he could fight no longer. This is where we sit in judgment of what happened next.

Understand something about General Lee. He was a good man and a Christian. He loved his home state of Virginia. And even though he took the unenviable position of defending a state that was pro slavery, General Lee was an exceptional human being. I am not trying to make a statement on slavery. I believe America should have found a way to abolish that primitive and inhuman practice when the United States was originally formed.

So here we are at the end of the Civil War. This is where the greatness of Robert E. Lee, and the course of America and the world, would be forever altered. When Lee surrendered, he did something extraordinary. He told the troops that the war was lost. He told them that there should be no more fighting. He told them to go home, rebuild and accept that the war was over. And because he was so respected and so beloved, his soldiers listened and complied.

America then began a reconstruction era. The social and economic problems of the south were not corrected overnight. There were Jim Crow laws, carpetbaggers, and segregation. One could argue that it would take another one hundred years before the playing field for all people in the South would finally begin to come together. So then, where is the greatness of Lee? It is hidden in the events that did not happen.

Imagine an America where southerners continued to fight from the hills. We could have been a country where terrorists, snipers, and guerilla fighters continued to wreak havoc across America for decades. It is not unreasonable to imagine that our healing and growth could have been severely hampered by this outcome. What would have happened in World War I if America wasn't there? Or if the Spanish American War didn't turn out the way it did? What would have happened if the industrial revolution was pushed back in America by twenty years? All of these would have been a distinct possibility if not for the pervasiveness of a general who lost a war.

There is no doubt that the lifestyle of the large plantation and the social structure that had been established in the southern United States was part of their way of life. It took the death of more wartime Americans than any other war to begin the process of erasing it and starting a new way. And even that process, being that it was mostly peaceful (with the exception of lynchings and the KKK), it still took one hundred years to develop. The depth of these events ran so deep into American culture that there are still hard feelings today.

I think it was very fortunate for America and the world that Robert E. Lee was the man he was, and that he had the moral character and the popularity to direct the new beginning for America. And the hardest thing to consider isn't what we experienced, but what we didn't.

What Do You Really Want?

ONCE UPON A time, in a forgotten kingdom a long time ago, there was an instructor who trained young people in the art of hunting. This instructor was appointed by the king himself, and he worked very hard to be the best teacher he possibly could.

Every year, he would get new students and he would teach them everything they needed to know for young men of their age. He took his job very seriously because he knew that when they became men, their hunting skills would make the entire kingdom a happier and more contented place to live.

He would teach them proper form, how to track, how to handle a weapon, and even how to read the weather. He was respected by the young men because they sensed his knowledge and admired his passion. In turn, the instructor was patient and kind to his students. He realized that he was showing them respect as young men because they took his lessons seriously.

The instructor would prepare every winter for the new class that would begin in the spring. He hoped that someday, the king would promote him to teach and lead the men on the hunting parties that the king sponsored every year. But year after year, someone else led the men while he taught the boys.

The instructor tried hard to define what it was he wanted to accomplish every year, and as he became more experienced as a teacher, he realized teaching the hunting skills was secondary to something else. He was teaching the boys how to be men. He would always say that you can learn more about someone by how they deal with the worst things in life than you will ever learn from how they handle the good things.

His new group of classmates would begin to bond right away. They learned teamwork and friendship; all the while they competed against each other. And most importantly, he taught them how to fail…like a man. His students that moved on would greet him years later because they knew he cared about them, and this made him happy.

He also enjoyed the idea that when they got to be fathers, they would teach their children the lessons he taught them. And even though the king went year after year with someone else leading the men in the hunt, he was happy to be making a difference.

Then one year, the food in the kingdom was running low. A letter from the king was delivered that told them to bring back as much food as possible for the kingdom during their training, and the instructor and his class worked very hard to make it so.

Then one day, the boys came across tracks of a large female deer. The boys tracked the doe to a small cave deep in the forest. When they finally had the large animal surrounded, they realized that she was tending to two small fawns. The instructor and the boys realized that this mother deer was alone as the men had killed her mate the week earlier. The instructor knew that it would be cruel to hurt this family of deer any more. So he took his class and left the mother deer and her young ones alone and safe there in the forest.

When the king found out that the instructor had left the deer alive, he was furious. "We have a food shortage and you let them go?" he hollered. The instructor tried to explain why it was the right thing to do, but the king wouldn't listen. He had the instructor whipped for disobeying his orders. The instructor's feelings were hurt more than anything else. He knew he did the right thing, and so did the young men he taught. In fact, they admired him for it.

The instructor continued to teach and just a few short years later, the lead hunter of the kingdom retired. The instructor thought this could be his big chance. He went to the king and asked if he might be considered for the job. The king said, "I will let you know."

A few days later, the king summoned the instructor to meet with him. The instructor put on his best clothes and bowed before the king.

"What have you decided, Sire?" he asked.

The king looked down from his throne and said, "I've decided that you are not fit to hold this post. I cannot consider someone who would disobey my commands for such a prestigious position!"

"I understand, Sire," said the instructor, who then bowed and left the king's service for good.

The instructor was very sad from this point on. He was so close to having the position he always wanted, but instead it was given to someone else. The instructor felt like a failure. "All those years of service just to see someone else moved ahead of me," he lamented. He felt like a dark cloud was following him after that.

Then one day, he met a lady at the market who sensed his failure. And she asked him what was bothering him.

"It is a long story, I'm afraid."

"It's a large market," she returned. So the instructor told her the whole story. Once he finished, the lady bowed and said, "Sir, you are looking at this all wrong."

With a quizzical look on his face, the old hunter responded by asking, "How so?"

"Were you capable of killing that deer in the forest? Would it have been the right thing to do?" she asked.

"Of course not; it would have been wrong," he answered. "So, in order to lead the hunt, you would have had to betray what you believe, and in front of the young men who admired you?"

Suddenly the instructor saw the bigger picture. He realized that he taught those young men a valuable lesson that day. And more importantly, he stood up for what he believed to be right—he defied the king himself to teach it.

The instructor thanked the kind lady for setting him straight. He learned a number of valuable lessons that day, the most important of which is "Stay true to yourself no matter what anybody says, because people are watching, and some of them might just be looking up to you."

The lady in the market had made a big difference just by taking the time for someone who needed it. The instructor wore a smile from that day forward. And if someone ever asked him about the king, he would very politely smile and keep his opinion to himself.

What Really Matters

A NUMBER OF YEARS back, when I was a younger man, I played a lot of men's softball. I was very good and so were some of the teams I played on. I would travel the northeast playing big tournaments trying to qualify for a World Series berth later in the year. I would also play a few local tournaments with friends to keep my skills sharp. If you want to be good at something, you need to practice to get there and practice to stay there.

There was one tournament held every year in upstate New York that we always looked forward to because it was set up exceptionally well. This annual event would gather somewhere around sixty-four to seventy-two teams from all over the state. The team that I played on had been going to this competition for ten years but had never been close to winning. They had made some improvements, however, and when they added me in, they had finally become a contender.

My first two years going there were a big improvement—second place both times. To win this tournament would give the fire district a four-foot-high trophy and quite a bit of attention at the tournament the following year. The final game would see close to a thousand people watching, and the atmosphere was electric. Adrenaline ran very high and every player there felt it.

My third year at this tournament started out very good. We won game after game by a large margin and we even beat the team that had won the tournament something like eight times out of the twelve years our district attended. The tournament is set up in a double elimination format, which means every team has to lose twice to be eliminated. We rolled right up and won the winners bracket. That means every team had one loss except us. Now we had to wait for the winner of the loser's bracket and they would have to beat us twice to win the tournament, but we only had to beat them once.

Late on Sunday afternoon, our longtime nemesis, which we had beaten the previous day, came through the loser's bracket and was set to play us again. How fitting it was, that to win the tournament for the first time meant we could secure victory over this team that had beaten us so many times before.

Both teams were very excited about this rematch, and the crowd and the noise were infectious. We played badly in the first game and lost. That evened everything up. The winner of the final game would take home the trophy. There was so much tension that a couple of the guys on our team who had played particularly worse than normal during the loss were actually crying in the dugout.

Our team had a number of great personalities on it, and by the time the final game started, everyone on the bench wearing our uniform was ready to win this thing for the first time. It is difficult to explain how intense the mood was. I can only compare it to the moment before a combat mission where the soldiers are scared and excited at the same time. Every player on our team was ready to explode.

The game started, and our guys jumped on top right away. We were up by about four runs in the third inning. We were not taking any chances playing against our archenemy. We wanted to score so many runs that it would break their spirit. We had two men on base with two outs, and another hit would lengthen the lead.

Our hitter stepped up to the plate. The dugouts and the fans were so loud it was just about impossible to not stand at the fence and yell like a psychopath too. I have played in thousands of games in my life, and there were very few times that ever compared to that moment.

But then, in the blink of an eye, everything changed. Our hitter drove a fierce line drive down the left field line that just cleared the fence. The ball hit a little girl directly in the head. The entire place fell silent. The only thing that anyone could hear was screaming. You could almost hear the air leaving the stadium as everyone in unison lost their adrenaline.

An ambulance arrived a short time later and took the little girl away. We were unsure of how badly she was injured, and once that tragedy was over, everyone looked for the game to resume. We continue on as best we could but the atmosphere wasn't even close to where it had been. We went on to win the tournament. We found out that the little girl was going to be okay. But the mood there was altered, and some of the guys were happier than others. I, for one, was not happy.

You see I realized something in that moment. I understood that the competition was fun and exciting...but ultimately pretty meaningless. I really hate losing, but I have lost my share. And I have a very strong desire to win everything I compete in. But I was brutally reminded at the peak of my excitement with that tournament that there are so many other things that are really important, like the safety of that little girl.

The emotion that I felt right then was shame. I was embarrassed that I had let myself get caught up in the moment. I learned a valuable lesson that day, and the lesson is this: Competition and games are fun and a good way to relax and recreate, but keep them there. And remember that life and the well-being of your fellowman is and will always be more important than any game.

Where Does the Devil Reside?

The Wolves Within (Cherokee Story)

AN OLD GRANDFATHER said to his grandson who came to him with anger at a friend who had done him an injustice, "Let me tell you a story. I, too, at times have felt a great hate for those who have taken so much, with no sorrow for what they do. But hate wears you down and does not hurt your enemy.

It is like taking poison and wishing your enemy would die. I have struggled with these feelings many times."

He continued, "It is as if there are two wolves inside me. One is good and does no harm. He lives in harmony with all around him and does not take offense when no offense was intended. He will only fight when it is right to do so, and in the right way. But the other wolf, ah! He is full of anger. The littlest thing will set him into a fit of temper. He fights everyone, all the time, for no reason. He cannot think because his anger and hate are so great. It is helpless anger, for his anger will change nothing. Sometimes, it is hard to live with these two wolves inside me, for both of them try to dominate my spirit."

The boy looked intently into his grandfather's eyes and asked, "Which one wins, Grandfather?"

The grandfather smiled and quietly said, "The one I feed."

There are many philosophies that discuss the nature of "right and wrong." Some of these are based on simple principles, such as "treat others the way you want to be treated" to more complex theories such as the eightfold path of Buddhism. Some people approach "right and wrong" by "feel." Others, sad to say, ignore it altogether. "Right and wrong" is more than a religious principle; it is also a social principle. To expand on that, think of people that you know who don't have a religious bone in their body but still follow an idea of "right and wrong." The truth is, even without God, human society demands that you conform to its principles or be looked at in a negative way. And people want to be accepted in most cases, so they conform.

One very common self-description in today's world is: "I'm a Christian, but I don't go to church regularly." They define themselves as abiding by Christian ideals, but not by Christian worship. I think the reason for this is that the philosophy of "right and wrong," as defined by the Christian Bible, that is, the teachings of Jesus Christ, are accepted as appropriate guidelines. But the practices involved in following a structured religion are more than what some people are willing to commit to.

There are always extremists to any issue. Some go too far one way and others too far the other. Pick any issue and you will find radicals in either direction that appear foolish or irresponsible. "Right and wrong" have their extremists too. There are religious zealots on one end and brutal dictators on the other.

I do not normally support extremists on either side, but there is one religious extremist who, during my lifetime, has always fascinated me, and I confess I admired her passion to the point where I am still in awe of what she did. I am talking about the saint, Mother Teresa of Calcutta.

Mother Teresa died on September 5, 1997. She died five days after Princess Diana of Wales. Princess Diana and her death created a media circus around the world. I have always felt that it detracted from the attention Mother Teresa's death deserved. I have never in my life known of someone more dedicated to the sick and the poor than this lady. She gave her entire life to helping people, and most of them were of a different religion. It makes me wish I could give of myself like that, but it is far more than what I am capable of.

There was a story I was told in college by one of my professors that went like this: During the fighting in Lebanon in the 1980s, a number of poor townspeople were trapped in the "no man's land" between the two opposing forces. Mother Teresa requested a meeting with the people in charge of the western side. She wanted to go in with her order to give medical and religious aid to the people trapped inside the shelling. When the military people asked her why she felt a need to go in there, she replied, "I have to go...Jesus is in there!" The military people did not understand. She explained, "I serve Jesus, and I believe that Jesus resides in the heart of all people."

They turned to the priest who was at the meeting and said, "Where does Jesus reside?" and the priest shrugged.

I have struggled with this idea for a large part of my life. You see, I have known a number of people who don't seem to have one attribute of Jesus within them. I have read about evil people all around the world, and all through time, and the actions of these people do not support Mother Teresa's belief. So does that mean that Mother Teresa saw something in humanity that I cannot see? Or does it mean that I see an aspect of the world that she refused to acknowledge?

And then that leads me to the next step to consider. If she is right and Jesus resides in the heart of all people, then where does the devil reside? Let me put the bigger picture away for a second and just consider myself. Does the devil reside in me? Or is it something on the outside trying to get in? Am I capable of terrible things? Could I become evil? This is a horrible premise; something I cannot accept. But if I could believe that the love or essence of Jesus is within all people, then I think I also have to acknowledge that the devil is in there too. It seems shallow and childish to say Jesus is within the heart of all people but the devil is not.

This brings me to this conclusion: That just like with "The Wolves Within," Jesus may be in the hearts of all people, but then so is the devil. And the one that you bring with you to the kitchen table is the one you let out. Maybe Mother Teresa was not wrong, but I don't think she looked at the world with the same practicality that I do.

It is always easy to find flaws with someone else's perception. But I will judge Mother Teresa not by what she said but by what she did. And there is no negative side with what she did with her time here. She served humanity her entire life. She asked for very little for herself. And so maybe that is the trick in life—to bring out the Jesus in people by being an example, and by keeping the devil buried inside.

The world needs people like Mother Teresa, not because we are all capable of doing what she did with her life, but by reminding us of what is possible. In my lifetime, few people have been so inspiring. I miss her.

The Sounds at the Tire Swing, Part 2

OPIE LOOKED AT the figure on the hill and immediately felt a deep fear. His worst nightmares were being thrust upon him. As the flash of lightning faded and the image disappeared, the picture in his mind remained as if it was burned into an old computer screen. He instinctively began to take steps backward away from the large dog on the hill. He wanted to go to the phone and call the phone number that he had taken from the news broadcast, but his eyes remained fixed on the glass. He looked down and realized that he had unknowingly removed his .45 and had it pointed at the large window that led out back toward the tire swing. He stood there, transfixed on the glass, waiting. His hand was shaking as if he was expecting the animal to crash through and into his house at any moment, but that moment never came. His attention to the window was finally broken by a strong smell of urine that was coming from the corner of his living room where his dogs, Katie and Kelly, lay huddled together shivering in fear.

Opie picked up his telephone and realized right away that it was dead. Moments later the lights, the TV, and the refrigerator went off as the power to his house was lost. *Blasted storm!* he thought. The sky was supposed to be getting lighter at this time of the morning, but because of the thick cloud cover, sunrise appeared to be on hold. He had thought the storm was ending but now he realized it was getting worse rather than better.

He went in his bedroom and got his cell phone. Luckily that still worked. Opie called the number that he had gotten from the TV news show and explained how he had seen the missing boys the evening before. He gave his name and address, answered a few more general questions, and the policeman on the other end said that someone would be out shortly.

Sitting there in the dark was the worst time for Opie. He hated waiting. He sat by the big sliding glass door which faced his backyard with his revolver on his lap. He studied the storm through the limited light of early morning. He watched the rain and the wind. The trees on the east side of his property were bending and bouncing under the force. Healthy leaves would be set free and the storm showed no real sign of letting up.

Opie looked for any kind of movement out there that did not belong. His visibility was limited because of the debris and the moisture in the air. He became lost in thought while he kept watch. His focus was finally broken by a knock on his front door.

It had taken nearly forty minutes for the two young policemen in raingear to arrive at his house. "Power lines are down a view blocks from here. Power crew just showed up," said one of the officers. "Are you Mr. Oppenheimer?"

Opie nodded yes and said, "That's right. Come on in, fellas." Opie did not immediately recognize either of them. The police force had so many new guys now and he felt like most of them were too young for him to know. But once he read the name tag on the shorter of the two officers, he realized that one of them was the son of a friend of his. "Barnes? You're not Jake Barnes's kid, are you?" Then they briefly reminisced while Opie got his raincoat on. Opie did not know Officer Pine but they both seemed like fine young policemen.

The sky was lighter now but it was still raining hard. Opie led the two officers out the front door and around his house to the path. He explained how he had seen the five boys walking in this direction the evening before. He told them he knew two of the boys. He was almost yelling to make sure that his voice could be heard over the sound of the wind. The three flashlights made their way down the path, over the hill, and to the stream. The tire swing and the old maple tree looked the same but somehow now they had an ominous quality because of the storm. Even the stream seemed angry in the hard rain.

The footprints and the animal tracks were all but washed away due to the weather. Opie and the two officers scanned the bank on the north side of the stream. They decided to eliminate this side of the stream first of all its clues. None of them were looking forward to crossing the stream to the tire swing in this weather. There didn't seem to be any kind of evidence of the boys in their initial search, and Opie was frustrated. He also remained on the lookout for the large dog that he had seen out his window.

Officer Pine came up to Opie and asked, "Is there any place near here that the older kids would hang out?"

Opie was embarrassed that he hadn't asked himself that very question. He suddenly felt very old. "The older kids have a spot just upstream where they make camp." The three of them followed the stream and trudged up a slight muddy hill with Opie in the lead. The hard rain and the stiff wind made it difficult for the three men to walk up the incline.

Once they got to the top, they turned away from the stream and went down between a short pyramid-looking pile of rocks and into a type of circled opening. There were still footprints here in the mud and some very noticeable animal tracks. Officer Barnes kneeled with his flashlight to get a closer look. "This dog must be huge! These are the biggest dog tracks I've ever seen!" he exclaimed.

Officer Pine looked down at the tracks. "My God…I think these are wolf tracks!"

Opie looked at the young man through the rain and asked, "What makes you say that?"

Officer Pine looked up from his squatting position while Opie shined his flashlight politely just below his face. "I go on hunting trips in Alaska once a year and I have studied the difference between dog tracks and wolf tracks. It's something you ought to know up there. Since dogs have a proportionally wider chest than wolves, the width of a dog's stride is greater. For the same reason, dogs place their hind foot beside their front, whereas wolves place their hind foot on the same line as the front foot. It is one of the only ways to tell the difference."

That sounded good, but Opie was not convinced. "There has never been a wolf sighting around here" he stated.

Just then Officer Barnes found some clothing. Opie thought little of it at first because the kids were always leaving stray shirts and jackets about. Sometimes Opie would pick them up and hang them on the rocks for them to find. Other times, when he knew the owner, he would take them home and give it back the next time he saw the youngster. But as officer Barnes began to hold up the wet clothes, Opie realized that this was different.

There was a torn shirt, a shredded pair of shorts, and a pair of torn boxers. After they looked a little more, they found a pair of sneakers. There didn't seem to be any way to associate these clothes with any one in particular, but the two policemen and the one retired cop all decided that they could be important. The three men decided to go back to the house and use the car radio to call for instructions. It seemed that maybe something out of the ordinary had happened here, and the officers wanted to protect the clothes as potential evidence.

About an hour later, a detective and a forensics team showed up at Opie's. The rain had stopped but the sky was still overcast. By 9:00 a.m., Opie was already tired. He did not get much sleep the night before. He was expecting the police presence down by the tire swing to die down, but instead, more and more people began to arrive. Opie met some of the fellows he used to know but most of them did not take the time to talk.

The retired police officer was becoming more and more suspicious of the whole ordeal. Then he ran into Jenkins. Jim Jenkins was probably his closest friend outside of the police force. He specialized in fingerprints. He nodded to Opie as he walked by but said nothing. Opie followed him down toward the tire swing but he was turned away by a young sergeant he did not know. *This is very unusual,* he thought. Opie was convinced that something was going on that he was not being told.

He decided now was probably as good a time as any to clean up the mess made by his dogs in his living room. Opie had just finished scrubbing his carpet when there was a knock on his front door. The detective and two other officers asked if they could talk to Opie for a minute. Opie decided that the detective had to have been a transfer from some other force, or he would have known who he was.

The detective wore a suit and a gray tie and introduced himself as Detective Mills. "This will only take a little time, Mr. Oppenheimer," he began.

Then for the next thirty minutes, Opie answered the same questions over and over. "Did you know the boys?," "What time did you see them?," "How big was the dog?," "What color was it?," "Where did you see it last?," "Have you ever seen it before?," "What time did you see it last?," and on and on it went. Opie no longer suspected that this was the scene of a horrible crime, he knew it was. He was also smart enough to not ask questions that they would not want to answer. It was obvious to Opie that whatever information they had, it was not yet released to the press.

Around 10:00 a.m., the interview ended and just about then his power came back on. The news channel on the TV was still covering the story of the missing boys but the content of the story had not changed. Opie decided to wander around a little bit outside in his yard. A news crew arrived from Channel 2, and they were not permitted to go down to the tire swing. Three very forceful officers prevented them from walking down the path. The news crews now knew that something was being withheld.

Not long after this, Opie's longtime friend Jim Jenkins came back down the path toward Opie's house. It was just starting to rain again and the people who didn't need to be outside began to head for cover. Opie discreetly turned to follow Jim out to his car. The fingerprint man went to his trunk and opened it up while

Opie circled around to the far side to attract the least amount of attention.

"Jim, how's it going?"

The fingerprint man never looked up. "Good Op… can't talk…people might be watching," he said.

Opie understood. "What's going on in my backyard, Jim?" he quietly asked.

Jim Jenkins still did not look up. "They found the bodies of the four teenage boys downstream. They were ripped apart. Now walk away, Op."

The retired policeman did as instructed and he crossed his front yard. Detective Mills watched Opie as he entered his front door. The rain made visibility a little difficult once again. And because of the rain and the distance, the detective was unable to see the tears that ran down the retired police officer's face.

The Oath, Part 2

WAHYA AWOKE AND was ready to begin the nightly hunt. The warm, dry air of summer carried with it a smell of flowers and dust. Wahya quickly got to his feet as a fleeting scent of a doe in its season hit his nose. As the leader of this pack of wolves, Wahya knew that a large meal during the lean days of summer were rare indeed. He scanned the den and saw only his mate with their litter sleeping comfortably in the early morning light.

He stepped outside and looked around and was puzzled by the emptiness. He deliberated within himself on waking his mate for information but decided to take a short walk instead. The opportunity to pursue the doe that he had smelled earlier was fading quickly. It didn't take long for him to get the information he sought.

He heard the sound of the other wolves approaching through the undergrowth of the forest. *Did they go on the hunt without me?* he thought. Soon the eight wolves entered into the clearing and approached him in single file. Lobo nodded to Wahya in the customary way to say "You are the leader." Wahya nodded back and smelled his friend.

"Where have you been?" asked the large wolf.

Lobo hesitated but only for an instant. "We went to help our cousin, the fox."

Wahya seemed surprised by the response. "With what?" he asked.

Lobo seemed less comfortable with his next answer. "He and his friends were being pursued by the great owl and his family."

Wahya was confused now. "What friends?"

Lobo told Wahya the whole story. He did not understand how the fox had friends that were not fox. He also was unhappy that he had been sidestepped by his cousin. The fox purposely asked Lobo because he knew Wahya would have been less likely to help him. *After all,* thought Wahya, *why help a rabbit when you could eat him instead?*

The morning sun rose on the large oak tree. There off in the distance sat the fox. Next to him were a rabbit, a turtle, and a mouse. Wahya sat at the edge of the clearing and stared at the spectacle. He could hear an annoying cardinal singing somewhere in the branches of the tree. It looked to him as if someone was playing a joke. He would never have thought to see such a thing. He stood up on all fours and slowly walked toward the old oak. All of the animals saw him approach. The brittle grass cracked under his feet as the dry, hot summer had turned most of it to hay. The fox tried to calm his friends and walked toward the large wolf that drew near.

The fox stopped and politely bowed his head to the leader of the pack. "Good morning, cousin," said the fox. Wahya sat down but said nothing. He stared at the fox and waited for him to explain. The fox was a sly thinker and quickly understood what the wolf was waiting for. "I apologize for not getting your permission, cousin. There was too much at stake and it was the only way to save my friend." The large wolf still said nothing.

The fox was not afraid but he was concerned. He liked being close to the wolves, and if Wahya was mad at him, he might lose their friendship. "I swore an oath," continued the fox. "They needed me, and I needed help."

Wahya signed. "Fox, I do not understand you. You swore an oath to them? Why would you do such a thing? And could you tell that annoying bird to stop making that awful sound? It hurts my ears."

The fox yipped and the cardinal became as quiet as the mouse.

The wolf sneered. "You should spend more time with your own kind and less time playing with your food."

The fox laughed. "They are my friends. They would be there for me if I needed them just as I would be there for them." It all sounded silly to the large wolf.

"Fox…do not trouble my pack with these problems of yours. We missed out on a nice meal this morning because no one was with me. Food is scarce during a long, hot, dry summer such as this. Respect my wishes."

The fox nodded. "I will, Wayha!"

The large wolf stood and looked at the animals clustered under the large oak tree. He almost wanted to laugh. "Good day, cousin." And with that, the large wolf went back to his den.

A few days later, the sky turned dark overnight and a loud thunderstorm passed close by. Wahya awoke and he and his family watched as lightning lit up the forest. The storm passed through quickly and the heat and the dryness of summer barely knew the difference. It was still an hour or so before sunrise when an annoying sound filled the large wolf's ears. Wahya awoke again to find that annoying cardinal in his den chirping frantically. He snapped to his feet quickly and began to growl.

The cardinal flew outside and then chirped even louder. Wahya had grown tired of the noise when suddenly he realized something was wrong. The forest was glowing all around the den. Soon the wind direction changed and smoke filled the air. Lobo came sprinting down the path from the east and yelped. "Fire! Wayha! The forest is on fire! I think we are trapped." Wahya's mate and their pups ran out of the den, and the little ones began to whimper.

Wayha thought of heading north over the hill, but if the path was blocked, they would all surely die. They only had one chance to guess the right direction but the glowing appeared to be all around them. The dry grass and the dry trees were helping the fire to spread at an alarming speed.

The cardinal flew back and forth and chirped as loud as he could. Wayha was trying hard to ignore him when suddenly he saw his cousin's face in his mind saying, "They are my friends. They would be there for me if I needed them just as I would be there for them." The large wolf turned upward and looked at the red bird who was frantically trying to get his attention. "Cardinal!" he said. "Which way do we go?" The little bird yelled as loud as he could "West! West! And then north to the river!" Wayha decided to trust the bird with the lives of his family and his pack. He ordered all of them to follow the cardinal.

The wolves ran as quickly as they could. Wayha brought up the rear to make sure that all of his pups moved fast enough. The fire was rapidly closing in on them. He realized that if the cardinal had not warned them, none of them would have escaped.

The smoke was getting thick and it became hard to see. Wayha had lost sight of his family as the blackness clouded his vision. The large wolf had no choice but to push on the direction he was following. He turned north to the river and he cleared the last small ridge to show the water and the forest animals gathering by the riverbank. The turtle sat on a log with the little mouse on his back. The fox, the rabbit and the cardinal stood by the river as the wolf pack assembled near the riverbank.

Wayha found his mate howling frantically as he sprinted toward her. "One of the pups is missing!" she lamented. "No, no, no!" she cried.

Wayha looked at his cousin, and the fox saw the deep sadness in his eyes. The fox began to yip loudly, ignoring that the smoke and the heat of the forest fire which burned only a few yards away. Just then he was interrupted by a tree which came crashing down in that instant only a short distance from them.

"Cardinal! Cardinal!" yelled the fox.

The red bird instantly darted back into the smoke and flames from the way that they had arrived. He flew in low and fast and within seconds his color and his song had disappeared into the abyss. The fox and the large wolf followed close behind and the three of them were swallowed up by large forest fire. It almost looked as if they were consumed by a monster who only moments later gave no indication of where they had even gone in. Wayha's mate continued to howl while the forest animals waited for a miracle.

Minutes past and hope began to wane. The little mouse trembled in fear. The turtle pulled his head inside his shell so that no one could see the look of sadness on his face. The rabbit sat upright and stared at the smoke. His great eyesight was riveted and attenuated to any movement with the blackness. He searched for a clue, a sign...something to give them hope.

Time continued to pass and the heat and the fury of the fire became so intense that most of the animals retreated into the water or onto the rocks that protruded from the river. Wayha's mate was now inconsolable at the thought that her once-happy life was instantly transformed into a nightmare of pain. It was a pain that would consume her, and the other members of the pack had to restrain her from running into the fire herself.

Then with a muffled cough and a whimper, the fox emerged from the black smoke with a wolf pup hanging from his mouth. He staggered to the edge of the river and then collapsed into the water. His fur was black and singed. The wolf pup yipped as it splashed into the safety of the cool liquid. Its eyes were closed from the burning effects of the smoke but soon, as the river water washed his face, his eyes opened to see and feel the loving tongue of his relieved mother.

And then, with almost no hope left within the pack, Wayha jumped out of the smoke onto the riverbank. He stepped toward the log where the rabbit, the fox, the mouse, and the turtle sat. And from his huge jaws, he laid the body of the bright-red bird on the edge of the water. The large wolf stepped back, reared up his great shoulders and gave a howl that could be heard for miles.

The sound of his cry drowned out the terror of the forest fire. It overshadowed the black smoke cloud and it pushed back the importance of the heat and the flames and all anyone could see, or hear, or know was the force of his body as it heaved forth with a wail that none had ever heard before. The rest of the pack closed in on the fallen bird and joined the lament. It was a spectacle that the animals of the forest would remember their whole lives. Animals that weren't even there would speak of it and say that they heard it miles away. It was told by families of the bear and of the beaver. The deer and the moose remembered it. The great owl and his family heard it from their mountaintop. And even the world of man would remember that day.

But it didn't end that way. The sound forced heaven itself to respond. The hand of God reached down to earth and restored life to the fallen bird. The cardinal stood up and looked around at all the attention he was receiving. He was unable to sing from all of the smoke. But the look on the faces of the animals that were there told the story. He looked into the eyes of the mouse, the rabbit, the turtle, the fox, and the large wolf, and he knew that he had made a difference.

A few days later, it rained again, and this time it was enough to help nature forget about the fire that had changed so many lives. New growth sprung from the old, and the burnt forest started anew, with new trees and new leaves for other generations to enjoy. Such it has been on earth for thousands of years.

A few days later, the fox was called to meet with the large wolf. The fox entered into a clearing to see Wayha sitting out in the open while his pups wrestled in the tall grass near the old oak tree. The fox approached and sat down next to him. The large wolf turned and nodded, acknowledging his presence.

The fox said, "You wanted to see me, cousin?"

The large wolf sighed a deep, heavy sigh. "I understand now!" he said. The two of them sat in the sunshine next to the old oak and watched the pups playfully biting each other.

"They sure are cute!" said the fox.

The large wolf nodded. "They sure are!... Thank you!"

The fox smiled. The wind blew slightly and the grass bent down with the pups as they tumbled to the ground. The clouds raced like turtles across the sky, and the cardinal sat on a branch in the old oak tree and sang his favorite song.

CPSIA information can be obtained at www.ICGtesting.com
Printed in the USA
LVOW12s1318190514

386416LV00008B/43/P

9 781630 638276